"You don't frighten me."

"Don't I?" Zane asked, his voice dangerously soft. "Then allow me to try again. Because it's easy to see that it's the most basic of things that scares you."

He reached out and grasped her upper arm.

Kelly gasped at his touch, at the intensity of his voice. Reluctantly she raised her eyes to his.

"Brace yourself, Miss Cordiner," he warned in a silky whisper. "You're about to be terrified. By an expert."

Then he took her in his arms and stared into her eyes. Kelly gazed back, her heart beating against her ribs like an imprisoned bird. She felt paralyzed, hypnotized.

When she didn't resist Zane lowered his face to hers and kissed her with a ferocity that would have been terrifying had it not been so achingly sweet.

Bethany Campbell, an English major and textbook consultant, calls her writing world her "hidey-hole," that marvelous place where true love always wins out. Her hobbies include writing poetry and thinking about that little scar on Harrison Ford's chin. She laughingly admits that her husband, who produces videos and writes comedy, approves of the first one only.

Bethany received the 1990 Maggie Award for her Harlequin Romance #3062 *Dancing Sky*. It's just one of this talented author's many romances to have delighted readers around the world.

Books by Bethany Campbell

HARLEQUIN ROMANCE

HARLEQUIN INTRIGUE

SPELLBINDER
Bethany Campbell

Harlequin Books

TORONTO • NEW YORK • LONDON
AMSTERDAM • PARIS • SYDNEY • HAMBURG
STOCKHOLM • ATHENS • TOKYO • MILAN
MADRID • WARSAW • BUDAPEST • AUCKLAND

To Paul McCluskey, for Pete's sake.
And to Dan Borengasser, for love of Pete.

ISBN 0-373-03187-4

Harlequin Romance first edition April 1992

SPELLBINDER

CHAPTER ONE

THE ROAD, red and dusty, wound tortuously between trees so thick that their limbs arched above it in a ragged canopy. Although the June day was hot and the Arkansas sun blazed at its zenith, little sunlight filtered through the thick foliage.

Tall ferns flourished at the road's edge, and once Kelly had to brake sharply—a white-tailed deer sprang out of the woods, bounded in front of the Jeep, then disappeared into the forested ravine on the road's other side. Kelly's heart had pounded wildly for a moment. She was a city person. She had never seen a deer in the wild.

The road climbed laboriously upward for a time, then twisted down at an angle just as steep. At last, near the bottom, she spotted a rusted metal gate with a sign that said Keep Out—Private Property. Kelly stopped the Jeep, although the gate stood wide open.

How like Jimmie, she thought, shaking her head in wry affection, to post a Keep Out sign, but not to close the gate. She knew he had a new watchdog, but it was overly friendly and never barked.

Jimmie had found the pup abandoned and taken it home because he was softhearted. And that was just like Jimmie, too, to keep a watchdog that wouldn't bark, only wag. Some neighbor had been feeding the dog, as well as the myriad stray cats Jimmie had adopted; she would have to find the neighbor and thank him.

And she would have the somber task of explaining what
had happened to Jimmie. Kelly's smile faded and the tight-
ness of grief choked her throat.

Jimmie was her uncle. He had been visiting Kelly and her
mother, Cissie, in Cleveland. Jimmie was a strange, lov-
able but feckless man, and he had a problem—he drank. He
had come to Cleveland in yet another effort to get *and stay*
sober, and he had been doing well. Kelly and Cissie had been
proud of him, hopeful for him.

But one night while he slept, Jimmie's generous, complicated heart, always so easily touched and so easily hurt,
stopped beating. He was forty-four years old and he was
dead.

Now Kelly Cordiner had come to Arkansas to settle Jimmie's small estate. Cissie couldn't face the task, and besides, she could not take the time off from her job in the
children's department of the downtown public library. Kelly,
who taught first grade, had the summer off. It was logical
that she be the one to go, although her emotions were just
as shaken as her mother's.

Jimmie's house on the lake would be in shambles; Cissie
had almost guaranteed that. But if Kelly could sort through
Jimmie's things, clean the place up and get it ready to sell,
she could also stay in the house until school started again.
It would cost her very little, she could enjoy the beauty of
the lake, instead of the concrete of Cleveland, and she could
use the peace and privacy to work on her book.

My book, Kelly thought almost fearfully. She was twenty-
six years old and had already sold two children's books. It
should seem a promising start, but nobody had paid much
attention to either, and they had sunk out of sight as quickly
as pebbles dropped into the sea. She hoped her third effort,
a book of animal fables, would be different. The third try,
she hoped, would be acclaimed. Her writing was the dream
that sustained her, kept her strong.

Kelly stepped on the gas again and passed through the open gate. There, beyond a last stand of pines, was Jimmie's beloved lake, shining blue and serene in the sun. She drew in her breath with pleasure. Jimmie always swore it was the prettiest lake in God's beautiful green world, and perhaps he had been right.

Beyond the pines, tall grasses and wild flowers led to the pebbled shore, shaded here and there by flowering mimosas, magnolias and tulip trees. The lake was narrow at this point, and on its opposite side soared magnificent cliffs of pale limestone.

Three or four small buildings stood scattered along the shore. They looked like weekend or vacation houses, and all seemed empty at the moment. But Jimmie had lived there year-round and she had no trouble picking out his house.

Unfinished projects littered the yard: an old car that was not quite restored, a rusted boat that needed repainting, a half-built henhouse without hens, a small dock that needed to be repaired before it could be put in the water.

The shrubs were untended, the garden neglected; the clothesline drooped because one pole had fallen down. In the midst of the mess stood a small brown-and-white dog. The little animal watched Kelly's approaching vehicle with so much joy that it seemed she might actually wag her hind end off. Here and there cats lounged—two grays, two yellows and a black-and-white spotted one.

No question, Kelly thought—it had to be Jimmie's house. It was small, gray with dark red trim, but in spite of the surrounding clutter, it seemed to be in good repair.

She wondered if the gyrating dog wagged so happily because it recognized the sound of Jimmie's old Jeep. Her mother knew little about Arkansas because Jimmie had always gone north to visit; he'd never invited anyone south. In Cissie's mind, Arkansas was a mountainous southern jungle, not suitable terrain for Kelly's tiny Sprint compact.

She insisted Kelly take the Jeep so she could traverse the wild country.

But when Kelly parked and got out of the Jeep, the dog greeted her with such contortions of tail wagging that it seemed it was welcoming the long-lost great love of its life.

Some watchdog, Kelly thought scornfully, but she scratched the dog's ears, which made the animal nearly dance her heart out with bliss. She was an ugly little thing, mostly fox terrier, but she had an infectiously happy nature.

Jimmie, Jimmie. Kelly felt tears of affection sting her eyes. Who but Jimmie would adopt this dancing clown of a dog and try to pass it off as a guard? No one. She shook her head ruefully.

The five cats regarded Kelly's arrival with boredom or ignored it altogether. One lay on the unfinished henhouse and yawned daintily.

So this was where and how Jimmie had lived, Kelly thought. He had spent most of his adult life as far as he could from Cleveland and all other cities. He had fallen in love with Arkansas when he was in the army, in basic training.

After Vietnam, it was to Arkansas that he returned to forget the horrors of war. Jimmie's drinking had begun on a tour of duty and so had most of his other problems. He'd been wounded badly, losing one leg, much of the use of one hand and part of the sight of one eye. He'd lived on his disability pay and learned to make a decent living—when he was sober and the weather was good—as a fishing guide.

Kelly swallowed hard as she looked out over the blue water toward the towering cliffs. This was where he had lived his final years and it was where he wanted always to remain. In the back of the Jeep, in a small, square box were Jimmie's ashes.

He had always told Cissie that he wanted to be cremated when he died, and that he wanted his ashes to rest in the clean, blue Arkansas water he'd loved so well. That was going to be another of Kelly's tasks, and it would be the hardest, loneliest one. She strained to keep her emotions under control. She had always felt things too hard, too deeply, always struggled to remain in command of her feelings.

She stepped up the two cement steps that led to the long porch. The dog gamboled about her feet, maintaining a frenzy of mindless joy. "Well," Kelly said to her with a sigh, "I wish everybody were as happy as you. A fine world it'd be."

The dog actually seemed to grin. Kelly blinked in surprise. She'd heard of dogs that could smile, but this was the first time she'd seen one. The creature stretched her lips, baring a friendly flash of whiteness.

"Oh, Jimmie," Kelly said, shaking her head again, "only you could find a smiling watchdog. Only you." She tried to ignore the dart of pain that pierced her heart.

She thrust the key into the lock and opened the door. The west wall of the living room was a row of windows that overlooked the lake and cliffs. Furnishings were sparse, but there was a desk in front of one window where she could set her typewriter once she cleaned the place.

Cleaning, she saw with sinking heart, was going to take some doing. The decor of Jimmie's home could best be described as "advanced bachelor squalor."

Heaps of newspapers cluttered every corner. Discarded clothing was strewn about as if just thrown. Cardboard boxes towered with cans that Jimmie must have intended to recycle, and most of them were beer cans.

Old magazines and paperback books lay scattered everywhere, for Jimmie, like the rest of his small family, was an inveterate reader. He was not exactly the family's black sheep, more aptly its stray sheep, but like Cissie and Kelly, he never felt complete unless surrounded by books.

But such books, Kelly thought with distaste, picking up one. *The Bloodletting* by Farley Collins. She turned over

another, *Tales of Mystery and Horror,* edited by somebody
named Talon. She picked up a third, *Werewolf Moon,* again
by Farley Collins. She dropped it back onto the tabletop in
disgust, as if it were dirty—and perhaps smelly. Collins was
the most popular writer of supernatural suspense in the
country. Both Kelly and Cissie hated such books.

Poor Jimmie had seen enough real horror in war, Kelly
thought. What demons had possessed him to read of still
more? No wonder he drank, if he sat out here all alone and
read such depressing trash.

Besides, she mused resentfully, Farley Collins was precisely the sort of writer who made hardworking aspiring
writers such as her want to give up in disgust and despair.

Not only did he write these tasteless tales of terror, he
wrote them with no apparent effort. There was a new Farley Collins novel every year, and for several years he had
somehow produced two of the vile things.

What made the whole phenomenon more painful was
how well such rubbish *sold.* Kelly had barely made a thousand dollars on both her children's books combined. Farley Collins's books sold at such a colossal rate he probably
made a thousand dollars a day. It was outrageous.

She tried to shake away her negative thoughts. Both she
and her mother had loved fantasy to be beautiful and to end
happily. How could Jimmie, who had been a kind and sensitive man, love horror so much? It had always mystified
them.

However, his housekeeping, or lack of it, was not in the
least mystifying to Kelly. She knew what must be done. She
had to make the house sparkle, ready to be listed on the
market as soon as possible. She must do this for Cissie, and
in a strange way as an act of love for Jimmie, one of the last
she could perform for him.

There was a tiny kitchen area with a cupboard full of
mismatched plates, cups and utensils. The bathroom held an
old fashioned claw-footed tub but no shower. There was a

large, screened-in deck she loved immediately, for it, too, had a view of the lake, and a gentle breeze wafted through it, bearing the sweet scent of the flowering mimosa trees.

The bedroom was large, airy—and scandalously unkempt. The bed lay unmade; a small television sat on a cluttered dresser, but its cord was so frayed she would be afraid to plug it in. A clock radio had stopped running, although it was plugged in and the electricity was still on.

She shook her head again and ran her hand through her thick brown hair. Squaring her shoulders, she stepped up to Jimmie's smudged bureau mirror and looked herself in the eye, trying to steel herself for the emotional job ahead.

Kelly was tall, as her uncle had been, but too slim. Her slenderness and long legs gave her a slightly coltish, almost boyish figure.

She did not consider her face beautiful. Her chin was too strong, her eyes too deep set, her nose too snub. If she had any prettiness, she supposed it was only in her coloring, for she had a complexion that was the natural blushing gold of a peach. The blue-gray of her eyes contrasted dramatically with the gold of her skin and the gleaming chestnut of her hair.

She was the kind of woman that other women called "striking." She believed they were saying tactfully that her looks were unusual, but not pretty.

Her face looked dreamy when she read or when she wrote. It could be compassionate when her first-grade students needed compassion, stonily stern when they needed discipline, or warm and smiling when they needed love. Right now, looking at the reflection of disorder of Jimmie's house, she had a determined face, her firm jaw set at a deliberate angle.

She wore cut-off denim shorts and a pale blue T-shirt so she wouldn't have to change clothes before getting to work. She would unload Jimmie's Jeep, then pitch into this mess. The sooner she got it cleaned up, the sooner she could get to her own work, to her book of fables. She had such high hopes for the book that the prospect of its failure deeply frightened her.

Kelly liked teaching, knew she was altogether too fond of her students, but she loved her writing with the same passion she reserved for her small family.

To work, she told herself, pulling back her hair and twisting it into a bun, fastening it in place with the few pins she always carried in her pocket. She almost smiled at her image. With her hair pulled back so severely and with no makeup, she looked every inch the teacher she was—a young woman who meant business and who would tolerate no nonsense.

She spent the next three hours launching her first assault against the house on behalf of neatness. It filled her with wrenching regret to gather Jimmie's discarded clothes, but she did, stuffing them into empty bags she had found in a kitchen cupboard.

The dog curled up contentedly on the rug, watching, wagging and occasionally giving herself a ladylike scratch. Forcing herself to be businesslike, Kelly methodically stripped the bed, gathered all the towels, took the spattered cloth from the kitchen table and put them in the bags, as well.

She intended to drive to the nearest town, where her first stop would be for supplies, especially cleaning supplies. Her second stop would be at a repair shop to see if the television and clock radio could be fixed. Her third would be at the Laundromat.

Last, she would stop at a Salvation Army or thrift store to give away Jimmie's cleaned clothes. It would not be easy. She'd also give away his collection of horrible books, and that would cause her no pang of sorrow at all.

Good grief, she thought in distaste. Jimmie must have bought every novel Farley Collins ever wrote, and a grisly collection of work it was. She shuddered delicately as she filled two bags with the things. After touching them, she washed her hands because they made her feel creepy, as if she'd touched something unclean.

She made her last trip to the Jeep, balancing a bag of books in either arm. The dog followed her, wagging her tail rapidly, prancing in excitement, apparently hoping for a ride.

Just as Kelly bent to set the second sack of books in the Jeep's back seat, a pair of strong hands seized her roughly by the waist.

"Not so fast," thundered a harsh voice.

Terrified, Kelly felt herself being jerked backward from the Jeep. She dropped the bag of novels, and it split when it struck the ground, scattering books over the grass.

I'm being attacked! she thought wildly. Her most primitive instincts leaped to life. She slammed her elbow backward as hard as she could, jabbing into the man's rib cage. When she heard his muffled grunt of pain she hit him again, this time harder. He only clutched her more tightly and swore.

"Hellcat," he almost spat from between his teeth, spinning her around, imprisoning her in his arms. "Even stealing his books? That's a new low."

Kelly looked up into the rugged face of a large man who wore a blue chambray workshirt. An escaped convict, she thought, dazed with terror. Clean-shaven and almost clean-cut, but most certainly a dangerous man.

She drew back her fist to smash it against his stubborn-looking jaw, but he laughed bitterly and pinned her against the Jeep so hard that she couldn't move.

He brought his face nearer to hers. His eyes, she saw, were dark gray and flashed with anger.

"My God," he said in disgust. "You're even taking his clothes? And the TV? And the Jeep? Where is he, passed out in there?"

Kelly, hardly hearing what he said, tried to kick him. He pinned her more firmly against the side of the Jeep, his long thighs pinioning hers, immobilizing her. His hands gripped her more roughly still, and he gave her a quick shake, so hard it momentarily jarred all rational thought from her head.

"Steady," he warned, lifting an eloquent eyebrow. "Don't make me hurt you. Just put everything back where you found it. You can start by picking up his books."

The dark gray eyes studied her in anger. They were astoundingly cold eyes. "I'll give him credit. At least he got a young and pretty one this time. But why you're sinking to this, kid, is beyond me."

He gave her another shake, the kind an adult might give a particularly fractious child.

"Don't try to hit me, don't try to kick and don't try to run. Just pick up the books. Put everything back where it belongs. The poor devil's drunk again, isn't he?" His nostrils flared, and he shook his head in frustration. "I didn't even know he was home again. This always happens. He always manages to meet a woman. And she's always the wrong one." He swore again, but he released her.

Kelly stared up at him in outrage and slowly growing comprehension. "Do you think I'm *stealing?*" she asked in disbelief. She rubbed her arms where he had gripped her. He had been none too gentle.

"He gets drunk," the man said, his disgust with her clear. "He picks up women. Then they steal him blind. It's always happening. You weren't the first to think of it, kid. Now pick up his books. Pick them *up.*"

"I wasn't stealing this trash," she almost snarled, and she gave the nearest book a savage kick to show her contempt for it. "I was taking it into town to give it away."

"That's no way to treat a book," he growled, real threat in his voice. "I suppose you're going to give away his television and his Jeep, too. How much of his money do you have? You can put that back, too."

"I didn't take any of it." Never could she remember being so outraged in her life. Never. "And it's none of your business," she snapped.

The man put his hands on his hips. They were lean hips, hugged by low-slung jeans.

"He's my neighbor. I make him my business."

"Well, he's not your business anymore," Kelly said, glaring. "He's dead. He died a week and a half ago." She knew her words were brutal, but she could not forgive the man for scaring her, for manhandling her and then, the final and intolerable insult, for calling her a thief.

The anger drained from his face. A look of pain and disbelief took its place. "Jimmie's dead?" he said incredulously.

For a moment his obvious shock almost softened Kelly, but she refused to relent. Her shoulders hurt where he had gripped her, and her heart still hammered from fright and anger. "Yes," she said, rubbing her shoulder resentfully. "He died of a heart attack in Cleveland. At my mother's house. I'm his niece."

He shook his head, his upper lip curled as if in pain. "Jimmie's gone? I can't believe it. God rest him."

Kelly studied him, rebellion still festering in her soul. He dropped his hands back to his hips and seemed to will his face to go blank, emotionless, as cold as possible.

He was actually a handsome man in an odd way, she thought. He had straight hair, light brown and gold streaked by the sun. All his features were strong and well cut, but more remarkable for their power than their beauty. His was a completely masculine face, with gray eyes deeply set beneath the ironic arch of brown brows. The pale blue of his shirt set off the coppery sheen of his tanned skin.

He was an imposing man and it was no wonder he had been able to render Kelly powerless. He was big, with an athletic build, and the rolled-up sleeves of his shirt revealed arms taut with muscle. He was wide in the shoulders, deep in the chest, and he had a strong, corded column of a neck.

Now he eyed Kelly as steadily as she eyed him. The fool little dog danced around his feet in apparent joy at seeing him, and one of the yellow cats rubbed sensuously against his riding boot.

Some watchdog, she thought again with bitterness. The man had grabbed her, threatened her, and all the dog had done was to leap about him, wag her tail and try to lick him. Kelly had never hurt an animal in her life, but she had a strong desire to connect the sole of her shoe to the dog's happily wriggling behind.

"Well," the man said with a shrug. "I guess I owe you an apology. I'm sorry."

His face was still blank, unrepentant. Kelly didn't like that. If he had an ounce of decency, he ought to be on his knees, cringing as he begged for forgiveness. His coolness fed her growing outrage at him.

"You *ought* to be sorry," she said, and rubbed her arm again. No one had ever scared her so badly in her life.

Instead of looking contrite, he gave her a thoughtful smile that was suspiciously close to a smirk. "I knew he had a niece. So you're little Kelly. He always talked about you as if you were only fifteen."

"I was, the last time he'd seen me," she said coldly. "And I assume you're a neighbor, and from the way that silly dog throws herself at you I assume you're the one who'd been feeding this zoo. I suppose I should thank you, but forgive me if I don't—you went a little overboard on guard duty."

There, she thought with burning satisfaction. That ought to show him she wasn't a person to be intimidated by any man—no matter how large or powerful.

He held up a hand as if to warn her. His crooked smile grew more sardonic, and Kelly liked him even less than before.

"Hey," he said, his voice amused but even, "I have certain rules I live by. One is I apologize once for something. Only once. You can take the apology or leave it. But if it makes you feel any better, I'll pick up the books."

"I'd hardly call those things *books*," Kelly said, wrinkling her nose in their direction.

"I happen to think they're rather good," he returned with maddening calm.

"I think they're trashy and terrible," she said, refusing, on principle, to unbend or be pleasant. "And yes, you'd better pick them up, because *you're* the one who made me drop them. By *pouncing* on me like a psychopath."

He knelt lazily and began to gather up the books, stopping now and then to admire a particularly horrifying cover. "Listen," he said, not bothering to look at her, "maybe you don't know about your uncle and women—"

"I know my uncle had problems," Kelly said shortly. "Spare me the details."

He raised his eyes and gave her a malevolently mocking look. "Another rule I live by—never spare the details. He had one woman out here who actually stole the sheets off the bed." He shook his head and turned his attention back to the books. "The sheets off the bed. Lord, the women he could find. Never, not once, a good one."

She crossed her arms imperiously. "I'm not interested in his—his sexual misadventures. And don't speak ill of the dead."

He rose just as lazily as he'd knelt, and put the books into the back of the Jeep. Then he faced her, crossing his arms in a parody of her militant stance. "I'm not talking about his sexual misadventures. I'm talking about his loneliness. I hated to see anyone take advantage of him, that's all."

"How noble," Kelly said sarcastically. "So you leap on strange women. You bruise and threaten and insult them before you know a single thing about them. You would have

made a fine junkyard watchdog. Far better than this—
thing.''

She gave the dog a glance as disdainful as the one she'd
given the man. The dog was so pleased by even negative attention that she wiggled and waggled her hindquarters as
energetically as a hula dancer.

"Oh," he said, regarding the dog thoughtfully. "You
mean Fang."

"Fang?" Kelly repeated, incredulous. "He named this
friendly idiot *Fang?*"

He cocked his head and looked at her through half-closed
eyes. "He had a sense of humor. You, I take it, do not."

"I most certainly do have a sense of humor," Kelly retorted. She was simply in no mood to waste it on this man.
"Under normal circumstances, I'm a veritable riot—I simply never stop laughing."

His eyes traveled up and down her body with insolent
boldness. "Could have fooled me," he said, and shrugged
again. "Anyway, the dog is Fang, the big gray cat is Rio, the
small one is Pilgrim, the fuzzy yellow one is Chewy, the un-
fuzzy yellow one is Podkayne and the spotted one is Dinah.
I, by the way, am Zane Graye."

"Zane Grey?" she frowned, turning up her nose further
still. "Like the Western writer?"

"Almost," he said. "He spelled it differently. My grandfather liked his books and named my father for him. My
father, alas, did the same when I came along. I live up the
road a piece or down the lake a piece, whichever way you
choose to travel. I raise a chicken or two and a steer or three
and aspire to be a gentleman farmer."

"You may be a farmer," Kelly said out of the corner of
her mouth. "You still have work left on the gentleman
part."

"Ah," he said, raising one eyebrow. "You do have a
sense of humor. I gave you a straight line and you used it.
Very good. Now what else may I give you?"

Good heavens, Kelly thought with a qualm of misgiving. *Now is he trying to flirt with me?* He stood with his muscular arms still crossed, his eyes still frankly assessing and the insolent smile still on his mouth.

"You can give me some privacy," she said in her best schoolteacherly tone. But she realized she probably didn't look like a schoolteacher, and perhaps that was why he was staring. Her hair had come loose during their tussle, and it spilled down her back and over her shoulders in a chestnut tumble.

In her old cutoffs, her legs showed their golden length, and she had worked sufficiently hard that afternoon for perspiration to paste her blue T-shirt to her body. She had been breathing hard ever since he had surprised her, and he watched the rise and fall of her small breasts with disconcerting interest.

"I suppose I should give you time to cool off," he said with his crooked, cocksure smile. "How long are you going to be around? Just long enough to clear the place out and put it up for sale?"

"I don't know," she lied, because his change of mood made her nervous. After all, he was a stranger—she knew nothing about him and they were alone in these woods. All she had to protect her was one giddy dog that did nothing more ferocious than smile. Kelly suddenly felt threatened in a different and far more intimate way.

It was as if Zane sensed her growing uneasiness and rather liked it. The light that sparked deep in his gray eyes was more blatantly sexual than before. "Is that your semipolite way of telling me not to come back?"

"I suppose it is. What begins badly seldom ends well, Mr. Graye."

He took a step toward her. She cringed against the Jeep. She was not, in truth, an easily intimidated woman, but he was making her more nervous than she would have thought possible. Her heart racketed against her ribs like a thing insane.

"What begins badly sometimes leads to some very interesting developments indeed, Miss—"

"Cordiner," Kelly supplied. "Miss Cordiner. And I don't think I need any more 'assistance' from you, Mr. Graye. The time has come to say goodbye."

"Not quite," he said, taking another step nearer. "I think you'll need me for certain things. I think you're going to want me—quite a bit."

Her cheeks flushed at the suggestiveness of his words and the heat in his eyes that belied his languid smile.

"I certainly can't think of any reason—" she began, with an imperious lift to her chin.

But he interrupted her by reaching out and cupping her chin within his hand, which was large and rough with calluses. The movement was surprisingly gentle, but there was deliberate sensual allure in it, as well.

Her heart jerked almost painfully at his touch, partly in rebellion, partly in sexual awareness of him. *Too many emotions,* she thought wildly. A river of them seemed to course through her, trying to carry her away. *Control them!* Her body went motionless, rigid as a statue.

"I can think of lots of reasons you'd want me," he said, his voice a sardonic purr. "For one thing, if you knew Jimmie's wishes, you brought his ashes back. You probably don't know where he wanted them taken. I do. So for his sake, you'll need my help. I also have certain—items—of Jimmie's. He got taken advantage of and stolen from so many times he asked me to hold certain things for him. I have. Among them is his will."

"His will?" Kelly breathed, too conscious of Zane's nearness, the power of his big body, the almost possessive way he touched her face. "We didn't know he had a will," she said, so upset she almost stuttered. "We thought he

died—what do you call it—intestate? My mother's checking it all out now."

"Then she can relax," Zane said, leaning nearer yet.
"There's a will. I haven't read it. But I'm sure everything
goes to the two of you. You were his only relatives, weren't
you?"

She nodded, her heart racing faster than ever, bounding
like the deer she had frightened on the road.

"So," he said, his voice low and insinuating, "you'll see
me again. And one more thing."

He bent nearer still, and for one crazed moment she
wondered if he were going to kiss her. Instead he reached
past her into the back of the Jeep, for its door was still ajar.

He took the top book from the stack he had set there and
handed it to her. "You called your uncle's books trash. Have
you ever read one of these?"

Kelly's nerve ends quivered because he seemed to be
standing too close to her, and her fingers burned when his
fingers brushed them. "No," she said, reluctantly clutching the book. "I knew I wouldn't like it."

He shook his head, his expression both sensual and rueful. "You should make a point of trying new things—even
the ones you think you won't like. You might be surprised.
I have the feeling there are all kinds of pleasures you haven't
discovered yet."

Briefly, so briefly it was breathtaking, he touched her face
again. "I'll be seeing you, Miss Cordiner."

He turned and strode off toward the still-open gate. She
noticed for the first time how broad his back was in com-
parison to his narrow hips, how long and sure his stride.

For the first time, she realized a horse was hitched to the
gate—a dark, dappled gray horse with a bridle, but no sad-
dle. So that was why she hadn't heard his arrival, she realized, her thoughts still roiling. She hadn't heard the soft
hoof-falls in the thick dust of the road.

She watched as he unhitched the horse and vaulted effortlessly to its bare back. He turned the horse, looked back in Kelly's direction and tossed her a careless grin. Then he galloped away, seeming as much a part of the horse as if he were a centaur.

Kelly stared after him, her heart hammering in her throat, her body filled with conflicting sensations. She stared down at the paperback book he had placed in her hands. The cover was a sinister black, the title shining in silver script; *Her Demon Lover,* it read, by Farley Collins.

She shook her head numbly. "Jimmie," she said, as if she could reach his spirit and receive an answer, "what kind of person is that man? What have you got me caught up in now?"

Troubled, she stared up the road, but the rider had already disappeared.

Too many emotions, she thought again as grief and resentment and anger and surprise still congested her breast. Too many feelings—she had to control them. Control them. Oh, *control* them.

CHAPTER TWO

ZANE SLOWED THE HORSE when he reached the highest part of the road, and began the descent back to the main highway.

He patted the animal's neck and smiled to himself. She was a spunky thing, Jimmie's niece, and an uppity one. She had Jimmie's blue eyes, set at that same almost catlike tilt, the same short, straight nose. He wondered if she had his same crazy smile, infectious and almost too wide. If she did, he'd probably never see it.

He shook his head. All right, he supposed he shouldn't have grabbed the girl, but that's what he'd had to do to that woman last year, the one he'd caught trying to stuff half of Jimmie's belongings into the back of her car. She'd been the one who'd even tried to steal the sheets.

She'd been a big woman, tall and heavy, and when Zane had grabbed her, she'd landed a fist to his mouth so hard she'd chipped one of his lower teeth. He hadn't been about to take chances with this one, even if she was half the size.

But he didn't want to think about the niece, not really. He needed to let the news about Jimmie sink in. He hoped Jimmie's gentle, restless soul had found peace at last. He'd liked Jimmie, liked him a lot. He'd encouraged Jim to go to Cleveland, to try to quit drinking again. He'd hoped this time the guy would be successful, but Zane had doubted it. Vietnam had hurt Jim too much, mentally and physically.

Zane understood because he'd been there, too. Jimmie had been an idealistic young man who'd had his idealism and his body ripped apart at the beginning of those long nine years of war.

Zane had been the same kind of idealistic kid—even younger than Jim had been. He'd arrived for the war's ugly end. He, too, had been wounded, but his wound, unlike Jimmie's, was rarely seen. He carried one small white scar, almost invisible now, directly beneath his heart. Like Jim, he, too, had had his idealism shattered, and that, he knew, showed all the time.

He'd come out of that hellhole of a war cynical, and then things had happened to his family that had made him distrust human nature even more. But he had come out of it stronger, tougher. That, he believed, was due to luck. He might have been broken by it, as Jimmie had been. Jimmie was a good-hearted guy, too good-hearted, and Zane would miss him. Once again he commended his friend's troubled spirit to peace.

He sighed again. Once more he found himself thinking of the niece. He supposed he should have made a more elaborate apology, but in truth, the woman had irked him, working her way under his skin with the irritating prickliness of a stinging nettle.

It wasn't because she was attractive, because she wasn't *that* attractive, he told himself. It was the fact she was throwing Jimmie's beloved books out and the stuck-up, priggy way she had acted about it. He remembered her kicking one in contempt, and that memory rankled in particular.

And what was it she had said when she'd wrinkled that little pussycat nose up over the books? That they were "terrible," that they were nothing but "trash"?

Damn, after she'd said that, he hadn't minded taking her down a peg or two. In fact, he'd enjoyed it, and he intended to enjoy it again. It had amused him to find that if he flirted with her she froze, almost helpless, in her haughty tracks. It gratified him to see her superior facade destroyed by such simple means.

No, she didn't like being flirted with, didn't like it at all. Therefore, he would flirt with her. He wouldn't mind, either, because he actually rather liked those long golden legs, the small, perky breasts and the strange, almost haunting bone structure of her face. And skin, he thought, she had great skin. Like a peach. He almost wanted to take a nibble.

A pair of quail ran across his path, their little feathered topknots bobbing comically. He reined the horse in a bit, and mentally he reined himself in, as well.

Kelly Cordiner had her pluses, he thought, but she was not that compelling. Too tall, too thin, her jaw was too stubborn, her eyes too steely; she was too controlled in every way. She had a quick-enough wit, but he'd seen none of Jimmie's warmth and vulnerability in her, not an iota.

He squeezed the horse's sides between his thighs to signal it to speed up again. It obeyed and he concentrated on letting his body flow with the animal's powerful rhythms. No, he told himself again. He didn't like the niece that well at all. He'd give up her and a dozen like her to have Jimmie alive and back in his own house again.

Damn, but he would miss Jim!

ZANE GRAYE HAD SHAKEN Kelly only because he had startled her so badly, she told herself as she drove back toward Jimmie's house. That was all. But she still felt unsettled, distracted, even after hours had passed, even after she'd been to town, done all her errands and done them efficiently.

She was full of these quaking emotions, she kept telling herself, because she was a long way from home and still grieving over Jimmie. To tell the truth, she was worried about how Cissie was handling her own grief. She missed the familiar security of her mother and their own home. And,

as every summer, she missed her students and wondered
what they were doing, all those sometimes wild and wily six-
year-olds. That was the hardest part of a teacher's job—
letting go of the children.

Well, she had a job down here to do, and feeling lone-
some wouldn't get it done. She would just have to draw on
her considerable self-discipline, as her mother had always
expected her to do.

She'd bought a mop and two grocery sacks filled with
supplies. She'd dropped off both the television and clock
radio for repairs. She'd washed the household linens and
Jimmie's clothes, then she'd driven to the Salvation Army
store and had given away the clothes and books.

For a moment Kelly had hesitated and almost kept *The
Demon Lover*, but she had restrained any impulse to be
charitable about Farley Collins or horror stories in general.
She also resisted out of spite. She didn't want to do anything that would please Zane Graye.

Zane Graye, she thought, setting her mouth more
grimly—what an impossible name. The original Zane Grey
was one of the most famous writers of Western books who
ever lived. This man looked like a cowboy who'd taken a
wrong turn and somehow ended up in the South. A cowboy who raised chickens.

She supposed he was attractive, if a person liked the ma-
cho type, but she did not and never had. Her father had
been that sort, and he'd been such a disaster as both husband and father that Cissie had divorced him when Kelly
was three, vowing never to marry again. Kelly had grown up
hearing the litany of her handsome father's freewheeling
sins.

No, Kelly liked men who made her feel safe. They were
soft-spoken men, polite and nonthreatening. They were
never physically intimidating; indeed, just the opposite, they
were never very physical at all.

But Jimmie, bless his heart, had been a little like that silly dog of his—he'd liked everybody. Leave it to him to befriend some overgrown Arkansas chicken farmer, or whatever he was, a man with no more manners than a cockroach.

She gritted her teeth as she turned down the dirt road that led to Jimmie's. Zane was not the sort of person she could like, so she wouldn't begin to try. Besides, he filled her with a peculiar, buzzing nervousness that made her feel vulnerable and unpleasantly breathless.

She regretted that she would be forced to see him again because Jimmie had left "certain things" in his care. But she would get the will and whatever else he had, and that would be the end of it. She wouldn't have to look at his obnoxious face or talk to him anymore.

Well, she amended, it was his personality and not his face that was obnoxious. He had a nice-enough-looking face, but was not *that* handsome. His jaw was too long and far too stubborn. His mouth was too sensual, too irreverent and too quick to provoke.

His eyes were so deep set that most of the time he had a Clint Eastwood squint she found unnerving, and his nose was far from perfect. It was—she searched for the proper word to describe the nose's fatal flaw—it was too *masculine*. It looked as though it had been broken, possibly more than once.

No, Kelly thought, starting up the rise of the wooded mountain road. He wasn't the kind of man who attracted her physically, mentally, emotionally or spiritually. She would trade him and a hundred like him to have Jimmie back again. Her dear, lost Jimmie.

HOW ODD, thought Kelly after she'd finally unpacked her purchases and had started back to work. She had been sure she'd gathered all Jimmie's horror books and given them away, but when she'd cleaned out a hall closet, she'd found one she'd somehow missed.

This book was a hardback, not a paperback, but the familiar black cover with its silver script made her heart race with apprehension. She touched the slick paper of the dust jacket and read the title, *Her Demon Lover* by Farley Collins.

Why would Jimmie have two copies of the same book? she wondered uneasily. Why hadn't she seen this one before? She had thought she'd searched the closet carefully. It seemed that this particular book had returned purposely to haunt her.

Don't be silly, she told herself sternly. *Don't be superstitious, especially not when you're out here all alone like this.*

The book had been stuck in the far corner of the shelf; of course it had been hard to see. Still, she opened it with trepidation. The title page was inscribed in a bold, black scrawl: "To Jimmie—Best regards, Farley Collins." Beneath the signature was a cartoon, half comic, half grotesque, of a grinning skull.

Inside was a Christmas card with a simple winter landscape. It contained a typewritten note: "Jim—Never understood why anybody wants autographed books, but enjoy—Best wishes, Zane."

Kelly thrust the card back between the pages, snapped the book shut and set it facedown on the table. Troubled, she was unsure what to do with it. Hardcover and autographed, it might be too valuable to give away. And since it was autographed, perhaps it was one of Jimmie's more treasured possessions and that's why it had been tucked so securely away.

She had cavalierly disposed of the rest of his collection. Should she have treated the books with more respect, simply because they were his? How should she treat this one? Return it to Zane?

Gingerly she picked it up again. The back cover was filled with glowing reviews: "The Master of Horror at his Haunting Best..." "A magic potion of terror and desire, certain to cast a spell over all Collins's fans..." "He has achieved the nearly impossible, by creating a love story as beautiful as it is fearful—*Her Demon Lover* is a devilish good read."

She flipped to the inside of the back cover, where publishers usually printed the author's picture and biographical information. There was nothing except a laconic note that the reclusive and prolific Collins seemed determined to stay reclusive and prolific. No known picture of him existed. He was as shadowy, as elusive, as mysterious, as one of the phantoms that populated his stories.

Why was he so elusive, wondered Kelly with a twinge of irony, when he was so successful? If she had sold millions of books, she would be proud. Collins must be one of those eccentric writers who slave to achieve celebrity, then—out of sheer contrariness—decide to hate it.

Going into the bedroom, she set the book on the dresser. Perhaps she should try to read it, for Jimmie's sake. No, she thought. She wouldn't read it. She had her standards.

Hot and tired, she thought yearningly of a shower, wishing Jimmie's house had one. But, she thought, spirits rising, if he didn't have a shower, he had a lake—a huge, clean, sparkling one. The sun was not yet down, the sky was streaked with gold and pink, and she could go out and swim in the twinkling water until she was cool and refreshed.

She changed into one of her bathing suits, the one with the dark pink bikini bottom and black bandeau top, slipped on her thongs and strolled to the pebbled shore, carrying one of Jimmie's worn towels over her shoulder.

She draped the towel over a cedar stump, kicked off her thongs and waded into the water. It was deliciously still and cool, the bottom gravelly beneath her feet. The sun was sinking, spreading ribbons of cherry-red light across the shining water.

The little white-and-brown dog followed her to the water's edge, dancing and wagging frantically. Now the creature stood looking after Kelly with a bewildered expression on her homely pointed face.

"Come on in," Kelly said with a laugh to the dog. "The water's fine."

The dog seemed to weigh the wisdom of accepting the invitation. Tentatively she put one paw into the water, then swiftly withdrew it, shaking it in distaste.

Kelly laughed again. "It's only water. You act like a cat. Somebody needs to give you dog lessons."

Still the dog wouldn't follow her. The animal stood on the shore, and although her expression was troubled, her tail still wagged, as if by habit.

Kelly waded in up to her thighs and stood, shading her eyes against the sinking sun. From around a curve in the shore came a strange cry, almost unearthly.

Then her heart rose in wonder as an enormous bird, as blue as the dusky evening sky, flew low, skimming the water.

A great blue heron, she thought in awe. A magnificent bird, its wings spread almost seven feet across. She was even more startled when a second bird, just as large, appeared. She watched as they disappeared, gliding around another curve of the shore.

Kelly took a deep, happy breath and dove into the water, which had a chill so deep it was somehow sumptuous. She rose and swam out, using a sidestroke and glorying in the cool freshness of the lake, the rose-and-gold splendor of the clouds stretching over her.

The cliffs were beautiful at dusk, their stone delicately tinted by the changing sun, and the trees that crowned them were almost magically green in the fading light.

Oh, Jimmie, Kelly thought, swimming under the gilded clouds, *I understand you better now. No wonder you loved it here. No wonder you never went back to the city.*

She reached the cliffs on the far side and looked back toward the other shore. Shrubs and small trees almost screened Jimmie's house from view, and the other little houses, as well. All seemed peaceful; it was as if she had the lake to herself.

She dove and swam underwater by the cliffs, playing along their edge. Then, when the light faded to gray and all other colors vanished from the sky, she began the long swim back.

It was almost dark when she reached the shore, and she climbed out of the water feeling heavy with healthy fatigue and blissfully clean.

The little dog sat waiting for her faithfully, head cocked as she watched her approach with growing excitement. She jumped and danced in gleeful circles when Kelly waded back to dry ground.

"I haven't been gone that long," Kelly admonished, laughing. "And I'm not the queen of England. I don't think I'm worthy of all this celebration, dog."

She reached for her towel.

"I don't think you're very smart, either," a man's deep voice said. It was heavy with mockery.

Startled, she whipped around, instinctively clenching her fists. The moon had risen, and by its silver-blue light, she could see Zane's powerful figure, lounging against a large fallen tree. He was half leaning on it, and in the shadowy, natural setting, he looked perfectly at home.

"You!" she almost spat. Was the blasted man going to make a career of startling her? Did he think he was funny? "How did you get here? How long have you been here?"

"By canoe," he said mildly, and gave a nod to one pulled up on the shore. "I got here when you were on the other side. I mean it—it's not smart to swim alone. Especially at night."

She snatched up the towel and wrapped it around her shoulders, wishing it were longer and hid more of her body. The bikini bottom was cut high at the thighs, making her look leggier than usual. Somehow this man, without making a move toward her, without suggesting anything aloud, gave off a palpable aura of sexual awareness. She wasn't comfortable being nearly naked in his presence.

"I'm an excellent swimmer," she said from between clenched teeth. She managed to wriggle her feet into the thongs and wrap the towel around her more tightly. "It just so happens in college I was a champion swimmer."

"Where?" His voice sounded both jesting and menacing. "In a college pool? This is a big lake, kid. There's no lifeguard if you get in trouble. Somebody could come along joyriding in a powerboat, not see you and knock you to kingdom come."

Although the evening air was warm, she felt unaccountably cold, chilled from the way he watched her. It was too dark to see his eyes, but somehow she knew he was watching, watching closely. The moon shone on the streaked thickness of his hair and his high, flat cheekbones. It fell, as well, on the breadth of his shoulders and silvered his long legs.

He stood, restlessly moving his big shoulders. "I mean it," he said. "It doesn't matter if you're a good swimmer. Over the years, a lot of swimmers have drowned up and down these shores. Most of them thought they were pretty good, too."

"I don't remember asking for advice," she said.

Her heart had begun its senseless hammering again. *Control, control, control,* her mind begged of her body. What peculiar, unwanted spell did this man always seem to cast over her? She hated it. She tried to sound as cold, as unaffected by him as she could. "I don't remember asking you to come back here at all. Did you bring Jimmie's will?"

"Yes," he said, his face now slightly shadowy in the darkness.

"And his other things? The things you said you were keeping for him?"

He nodded. "I brought it all. I thought it should be turned over as soon as possible."

She held out her hand. "Then turn it over, please. Then you can go back wherever you came from. Sneaking up on me once today is bad enough. Twice is—intolerable."

He ignored her extended hand. He cocked one hip and hooked his thumbs in his belt. It was a militant stance.

"I didn't sneak. I came around the bend in plain sight. A canoe is quiet, that's all. You were too busy pretending to be an otter to notice me. I was here the whole time, keeping my eye on you. In case you got into trouble."

She took a deep breath and kept her hand held out. "The only trouble I'm having is you. Would you mind handing over my uncle's things?"

He reached into the canoe and picked up a backpack. It was large and looked heavy, heavier than she might comfortably manage.

"I'll take it to the house for you," he said, shouldering it. "It's got his rock collection in it. Among other things."

Kelly sighed impatiently. A rock collection. Of course. She loved Jimmie, but he seemed to have a genius for acquiring useless and troublesome items: a dog that wouldn't bark and a collection of rocks that she probably couldn't even lift. And the worst thing he had collected was this perplexing, unpredictable friend.

"All right," she said shortly. "Come on. I can't believe this silly dog didn't even bark when you came."

She turned and strode toward the house, the dog running in happy circles around her feet. Let Zane follow her as he would, she thought. How, she wondered darkly, did she easily manage a room full of six-year-olds of every sort of temperament, yet have such difficulty with one adult man?

She pushed open the front door and the dog ran inside as she stepped in. Before Zane could get through the same door, Kelly hurried to the bedroom, took her heavy peach-colored robe from the closet and bundled into it, pulling it close and belting it tightly.

There, she thought, her eyes narrowing. She was as thoroughly covered as if she were wearing an overcoat. Let the man try to stare at her now. She'd left little for him to stare at.

She stepped back into the living room just as he entered from outside. He crossed the small room and set the backpack on the table by the window.

She tossed her wet hair back from her face, and she knew the look she gave him was stony. "Thanks," she said frostily, and crossed her arms, waiting for him to go.

In the small house he seemed even taller, more powerfully shouldered than before. He wore the same faded jeans as he had worn earlier in the day, the same dusty riding boots, but his pale green shirt was short-sleeved and revealed how strong and sinewy both his forearms and upper arms were.

He looked at her, from the top of her head with her hair plastered to her skull, to the bulky lines of the robe, to her feet in the thongs and back up again. His face was as stony as hers.

He simply stood there for a long time, his eyes so intent he made her nervous. Her heart began to beat harder still, crowding the air out of her chest. *It's because of Jimmie,* she kept telling herself. *I'm feeling all these emotions because of Jimmie.*

"You're welcome," he answered at last. "A neighborly person might say, 'Since you went to all this trouble, sit and have a cup of coffee.' I take it you're not neighborly."

Suddenly she realized the glint in his eyes was partly amusement at her nervousness, and resentment flashed through her. He knew that he frightened her a bit, and he actually *enjoyed* it, the lout. She hated letting him have such an advantage and fought it with all her might.

"Sit," she said inhospitably. "You'll have to settle for instant coffee. It's all I've got."

He smiled. She was taken aback. He had a surprisingly genuine smile, an almost comforting smile. Although she mistrusted almost everything else about him, she thought with confusion, she instinctively trusted his smile. How odd. How paradoxical. She already regretted asking him to stay; he was too disquieting.

"When I meet a woman who knows how to make real coffee, I'll marry her," he said. "But I see I'm safe here. I'll sit." He pulled out a chair, turned it around backward and settled onto it like a cowboy on a horse. He leaned his elbows casually on its back and watched her as she bustled self-consciously in the little kitchen area.

"Maybe I can help explain some of the things in here to you," he said, nodding toward the backpack.

"Fine," Kelly said brusquely. She cast him a furtive glance as she turned on the teakettle. Was he menacing or not? Now, in the golden lamplight, she couldn't decide. His air could change with unnerving quickness.

"Your uncle left another copy of his will at a lawyer's. Over in Washington County. Ms. Phoebe Carrington. In Fayetteville. She'll help you make sure everything's in order." He frowned slightly, then reached down and scratched the dog behind the ears. The dog fairly beamed at him.

"As for Jimmie's other things," he said, the frown still in place, "they'll take some explaining."

She leaned against the kitchen cabinet, her arms crossed again, her expression carefully composed. The lamplight gleamed on the sun streaks in Zane's brown hair, made his deep-set eyes seem more shadowy and unreadable than before. Yet in repose, his strong face almost gave the impression of kindness, even possibly gentleness. Perhaps, she cautioned herself, it was merely a trick of light.

She was grateful he was paying attention to the adoring dog, not leveling his disturbing stare on her. She studied him, setting her jaw. "Why'd you do it again?" she asked softly. "Scare me again? Come creeping up in your boat and wait for me?"

He shrugged, not bothering to look up. He stared instead into the dog's brown, worshipful eyes. "I don't know," he said carelessly. "Maybe I thought you deserved to be scared—a little. You should be careful out here by yourself."

"That's no excuse," Kelly countered, pushing her damp hair back from her forehead.

He took his hand away from the dog and raised his eyes to hers. "The burned child fears fire," he said evenly.

Kelly wished his gaze didn't jolt her so sharply. She tilted her chin more defensively. "I'm no child," she said, and immediately knew it was the wrong thing to say.

He smiled, the curve of his mouth both amused and rakish. "I'm aware of that."

"Oh, stop it," she said irritably, pushing her hand through her hair again. She knew she wasn't sexy, so he should stop watching her as if she were. Her hair was wet, she wore no makeup, the oversize robe swaddled her as thoroughly as if she were wrapped in a bearskin and her feet were in rubber thongs.

She understood what he was doing, she thought with a surge of anger. He didn't find her attractive in the least. But he knew he could make her nervous by pretending to do so. He was teasing her, that was all. Teasing—as if she were indeed a child.

She looked away from him and stared out the window so she wouldn't have to look at him. The lake sparkled in the moonlight.

"Besides," he said, sounding unrepentant, "I told you. I came in peace, bearing gifts from your departed relative, and you were gone, frolicking around in the water like the star porpoise in a porpoise show."

"You came stealing out of the shadows," Kelly said a bit melodramatically, "like a thief in the night. Then you crept onto my uncle's property and *lurked.*"

He raised an eyebrow and nodded solemnly. "I *crept.* I *lurked.* I like the sound of that. It has a certain ring."

"Stop teasing," she ordered, still not looking at him.

"Why, when I like it so much? And you're so teasable?"

"Because it's not *nice,*" she said emphatically. "Stealing up on people and not announcing your presence is not *nice.*"

She glanced at him out of the corner of her eye. He was smiling so widely that he almost laughed.

"Have I ever," he asked, "in our brief relationship, expressed the desire to be 'nice'? 'Nice'—what a wishy-washy, weak-kneed word."

She turned her head to face him again, disgusted. "I think you *like* scaring people."

He gave her his most evil grin, and she wondered how she'd ever imagined his smile to be comforting. "I do. But only enough to make them happy. There's little enough happiness in the world. I try to do my bit to help."

The teakettle began to sing and she took it off the burner, shaking her head in frustration as she poured hot water into two mismatched mugs. He was an impossible man, and he'd raised self-satisfaction to a nearly perfect art. How could Jimmie have stood him, let alone trusted him?

She carried the mugs to the table and set them down with as much authority as she could muster. She pulled out the remaining chair and sat down, as far across the table from Zane as possible.

"And what's in the bag of goodies?" she asked sarcastically. "Besides Jimmie's rock collection? Did you put in some nice bats and spiders, just to give me a pleasant shock?"

"Ah," Zane said, sighing with feigned patience, "you don't understand. You don't even try. You have racehorse

legs but a mulish brain.'' He dug into one of the backpack's pockets and withdrew a sealed envelope. "Here's the
will. You'll probably want to read it in private.''

"Thank you,'' she said, giving him a sidelong look as she
took the envelope. "I'm sure you know what's in it already, however. Jimmie wasn't much good at keeping secrets.''

"I do know,'' he agreed pleasantly. "But don't under-
rate your uncle. He *was* good at keeping a few secrets.''

"Really?'' Kelly said, and opened the envelope. She
wanted to make sure only that everything went to her
mother, as it should by rights. She hoped Jimmie hadn't
done something foolish, such as leave half or all his worldly
goods to this smug man who claimed to have been his
friend.

She scanned the will, trying to skip over the legalese that
entangled its message. Her lips parted in surprise and she
frowned. "I thought he'd leave everything to Mother. He
didn't. He left part to me. He didn't have to do that. He
shouldn't have. Mother was his closest relative. It should
have gone to her. And he made me the executor.''

"It's his will,'' Zane said. "He apparently wanted to
provide for you, too. And he probably figured you'd be the
abler executor. Less emotional. Hardly any emotion at all,
in fact.''

"Well, that was sweet of him,'' Kelly said, ignoring his
gibe. She fought traitorous tears that wanted to flow in
tribute to Jimmie's generosity. He had left her a third of his
estate and the remaining two-thirds to Cissie.

"So,'' Zane said, "you have quite a legacy—what—a
fourth of his estate?''

"A third,'' she said, her face rigid as she struggled to
suppress the tears. Zane was the last man in the world she
wanted to see her cry. She rubbed her eye as if a speck had
irritated it.

"A third," he said, opening the backpack. "A third of whatever this house and land sells for—when it sells. Which may take a while. This is an isolated spot. Not everybody's cup of tea."

Kelly nodded. She realized that. The little house might not sell for months, maybe even longer.

"And you have a third of a twelve-year-old Jeep," he went on as he set a few arrowheads on the tablecloth. "And a third of a car that won't run, a boat that won't float and an unfinished henhouse. And this arrowhead collection."

Well, Kelly thought, rubbing her eye again, Zane's mocking tone made Jimmie's few belongings sound like a poor bequest, but it was Jimmie's thoughtfulness that counted, not how much he had left behind. Her lip trembled, and she bit it to keep it still.

She stared sadly at the line of arrowheads that Zane had arranged on the tabletop. She knew nothing of arrowheads.

"Even a tomahawk," he said, settling a larger stone beside them. "And some quartz crystals. This state's famous for quartz. Jimmie got some excellent samples. Excellent if you're into the New Age."

Kelly was interested in neither the New Age nor crystals and their mystic uses. She wished only that Zane would keep the effrontery out of his voice and that she didn't feel so unaccountably weepy, looking at these things that Jimmie had prized and wanted her and Cissie to prize, as well.

"Look at this," Zane said in sardonic wonder. "A genuine meteorite. Found in a field near Hog Eye, Arkansas. This may be worth something."

Beside the quartz crystals he set a large, irregular black stone, half the size of a soccer ball and obviously heavy.

"Hog Eye?" she said suspiciously, giving him a look that she hoped told him she was in no mood for jokes.

He held his hand up as if being sworn to the truth. "On my oath. A lovely place, Hog Eye. I think they named it that to keep the Yankees away. Anyway, there it is—Jimmie's meteorite. Lord, he was proud of that thing.''

Kelly was suddenly bone-weary and overwhelmed with sorrow. Zane's making fun of Jimmie's most treasured possessions seemed wrong, yet it held a justice that hurt. Jimmie had lived all those years and what did he have to love? Besides his little house and patch of land, nothing. Nothing except a pile of stones. Cold, inhuman, indifferent stones.

She couldn't stifle a slight sniff, and ran her hand beneath her nose as if she had inhaled water while swimming and now it troubled her. She set her jaw more tightly. She would not cry before this man. She would not. She felt him staring at her again.

"Sad that it's so little?" he asked after a pause.

"No," she said harshly. "Only because it was so little for him. This is all he had to love? A bunch of rocks?"

She put her elbow on the table and her cheek on her fist. She stared out at the lake again, watching how the moonlight played, silver, on the ripples. How peaceful it seemed compared to the turmoil she felt within.

"No," Zane said harshly. "He loved his books, too. But those, of course, you gave away."

Kelly stiffened guiltily, but kept staring at the moonlight glittering on the water.

"And you, of course," he went on, his voice still harsh. "You and your mother. He loved you two. Although I had the feeling you didn't always approve of him."

Kelly bit her lip harder. It was true. She and Cissie hadn't always approved of Jimmie. How could they? He was too self-destructive. But they had loved him. Even during long periods when relations had been strained because of Jimmie's drinking, there had never been any question that they loved him.

"He wanted your approval, you know," Zane said, his tone almost relentless. "He would have done almost anything to make you happy."

"Then he should have stopped drinking," Kelly said, wishing Zane would be quiet. She knew that if he went on this way she would cry, no matter how much she fought the urge.

"You wanted the one thing he couldn't seem to do," Zane said softly, his voice almost a hiss. "But tell me. What would your mother do if she had money? *Real* money?"

Kelly was tired of being pushed, teased and quizzed. She turned her face to him and didn't try to hide the tears that blazed in her eyes. "She'd travel. Will you get to the point? What business is it of yours? She always said she'd travel if she had money. What do you care? Get on with it, will you?"

If he noticed her tears, they didn't seem to register on him. He stared at her, his smile as wicked and crooked as before. "And where would she travel?"

"Hawaii," Kelly said angrily. "She always said she'd go to Hawaii. She says it sounds like paradise. *Why?* Look, I'm tired. I'm still upset by my uncle's death. I—"

He tilted his chair so he leaned toward her, his smile widening. "And you? What would you do if you had money? What's your particular dream?"

"I'd write," she said emphatically. "I'd give up teaching and I'd write—full-time."

"Write?" His smile grew more cryptic. "Ah, yes. Jimmie said you wrote. But I forget what. Children's stories?"

"Yes," she said, her patience breaking. He'd pushed her too far and she could not resist the urge to push back. "I would. And I'd write better books than that *tripe* Farley Collins writes, too."

The dig drew no reaction. His expression remained precisely the same, mysterious, yet satisfied. "You think so? Then do it, Kelly," he said, taking her hand in his.

In his other hand he held a small leather bag with Indian beading on it.

"What—" she said, objecting to his touch and trying to draw away. But he held her hand fast, palm up.

"Write better books than Farley Collins and tell your mother to pack her bags for paradise," he said, his voice softer than ever. "You're rich, Kelly. Well, not rich, but nearly so."

He tilted the bag, and glittering stones fell into Kelly's hand, so many they spilled over and landed, rattling, on the tabletop.

Kelly stared at them, then at him, as perplexed by his touch as by the shining pebbles he was pouring into her hand. "What—" she said again, staring into his unfathomable eyes.

"Diamonds, Kelly," he whispered, his hand folding hers tightly around them. "Diamonds. Among other things. A small fortune in jewels."

CHAPTER THREE

HIS HAND, clenching hers, was hard and strong.

"What?" Kelly said. She stared into Zane's eyes in disbelief.

His smile stayed in place. He squeezed her hand more tightly. "Diamonds. Also sapphires. And emeralds."

An eerie coldness clamped her spine at the base of her skull. She was almost glad that he held her hand. It was as if his touch kept the universe from turning completely upside down. "Jewels? Where did Jimmie get jewels?"

He leaned toward her more closely, putting both elbows on the table. He wrapped his other hand around her fist, as if using both hands either to imprison or protect her.

"Thailand," he said, obviously savoring her surprise. "When he was on leave from Vietnam."

She shook her head, incredulous, staring at his large hands locked around hers and at the glitter of the uncut gems that had fallen to the tabletop. "But—" she said, searching for words. "But—how—"

"Don't ask, Kelly," he almost purred, his eyes on her trembling lips. "I don't know. All he told me was that they were legally his. There's no crime attached to them. No stigma. I think it had something to do with a poker game. They're yours and your mother's, free and clear. He always meant them for this—his legacy to you—his surprise. He knew that the longer he hung on to them, the more they'd be worth for you."

Benumbed, she looked into his eyes. "Why didn't he use them for himself?"

"Kelly," he drawled, his eyebrow rising sardonically, "we're talking about Jim here. He wanted this little fortune to be yours—he wanted to leave you something. And he did. These stones."

"I—I don't even know one stone from another. Or how much they're worth," she said, gripping them more tightly. *Jimmie,* she thought, full of misapprehension, *all this time you were rich? Rich? But you saved it all for us?*

"He knew," Zane said, smiling more widely at her confusion. "He said about $300,000."

She stared again at his strong hands gripping her clenched one. Shock had left her feeling cold and helpless and she was grateful for the warmth and power that seemed to pour from his touch. Stunned, she unconsciously squeezed his hand against hers.

If the stones were worth $300,000, she thought dazedly, then Jimmie had left her $100,000. And her mother, a woman who had worked so hard all her life with so few luxuries to show for it, now had $200,000—a fortune.

"Right," Zane agreed, although she had said nothing. "I can see the wheels turning in your head—you're doing the math. Quite a windfall. You can take a year off if you want. Even longer. And write books. Better books than Farley Collins. If you can."

He released her hand, allowed his chair to tilt back into place. He sat a moment, his hands on his muscular thighs, watching her.

Still openmouthed in amazement, she could only stare at the dully glimmering stones in her hand. But her hand, she suddenly realized, felt almost weak without the support of his.

He grinned more crookedly and, swinging his leg over the chair, stood up. She raised her eyes to meet his. She felt vulnerable somehow, almost naked, in spite of her heavy robe.

"Tomorrow you'd better take them into town. Put them in a safety deposit box. As for tonight—well, I hope guarding a fortune in jewels doesn't make you nervous."

Kelly, her gaze fastened on his, swallowed, her mouth suddenly dry. Until he had spoken of it, it hadn't occurred to her that she would be left alone, a woman isolated in the woods, guarding an unsuspected treasure. She licked her upper lip nervously, and he watched the movement with lazy interest.

He put his hands carelessly on his hips. "Unless," he said, his tone throbbing with both suggestiveness and laughter, "you want me to stay. You said I'd make a good watchdog. I guarantee you, my bite is as good as my bark. And I curl up nicely in a bed. Warm, too."

She was almost more astonished by his proposition than she had been by the gems. As usual, he sent her emotions spinning off in a kaleidoscopic blur. In desperation she focused on anger. "Damn you," she said, her jaw going steely. "You're trying to scare me again. I can tell by the look in your eye. Why? Why don't you just let me alone?"

He laughed softly. "Remember I *like* to scare people. Harmlessly, of course. As for leaving you alone, I will—if you insist. But, given the circumstances, you might feel more comfortable if I stayed."

Under her breath, Kelly cursed him again. Still, she knew her face radiated as much surprise as outrage; everything had seemed slightly unreal since he had poured the jewels into her hand.

He cocked his head in mock disapproval. "Is that any way for a schoolteacher to talk? For shame. What an example."

He reached out, took the empty backpack and slung it negligently over his shoulder, like an unworn coat. "On the other hand," he said nonchalantly, "I wouldn't want you to get too scared. So I brought my sleeping bag. And my rifle.

I'll just camp down by the shore where I can keep an eye on you and your place."

She swallowed again. She didn't want him presuming he could watch over her, but she didn't want to be left alone with the jewels, either. "I can take care of myself," she said, her voice shaking with conflicting emotions. "I can lock the door, I can hide the jewels, and nobody knows they're here, anyway, except you. Besides," she said, grasping at straws, "I have a dog."

He laughed again. "I'll be down by the shore. If you want me, just step into the moonlight and call. And you *don't* have a dog." He reached down and scratched the terrier's ears again, which made the animal writhe and twitch with adoration. "You have *this*—whatever it is. Good girl, Fang. If any prowlers show up, don't love them to death."

He turned and walked to the door, his pace as easy as a big cat's. He shot Kelly a casual glance over his shoulder. "As I say, I'll be down by the shore. If you want me closer— well, it's easily arranged."

"I want you as far from me as possible," she said, her voice strangled.

He opened the door and tossed her one last insolent smile. "It's a good thing you gave away all the Collins books, right? This certainly wouldn't be the night to read anything to make you nervous."

He swung open the door and strode out into the moonlight. Kelly watched the door shut behind him. She licked her lips again, her mouth drier than before, her heart knocking crazily in her chest.

She picked up the small leather bag and poured the stones back into its depths. Then, clutching the bag, she rose and went to the door. She locked it and wished it had a dead bolt.

She was breathing hard, and her knees, she discovered, felt as wobbly as pudding. She returned to the table and sat down, staring, still dazed, at the sack of uncut jewels. The dog danced to her side and lay her head in her lap, gazing up at her in happy loyalty.

Kelly shook her head. She didn't want to look out the window. She was afraid she would see Zane's dark shape down by the shore. Somehow she knew he would be as good as his word. He would stay out there all night, guarding her and the house. It was a comforting thought, and at the same time disconcerting, not one on which she wanted to dwell.

She pulled the oversize robe more snugly around herself, then let her hand fall helplessly into her lap. The dog licked it enthusiastically, but Kelly hardly noticed.

"Dog," she said in wonder, "where did Jimmie get these stones? How did he hang on to them so long? Why didn't he spend the money on himself?"

There was one more question she didn't wish to utter aloud. Why had Jimmie trusted Zane, of all people, with this unexpected family fortune? Had he really trusted and respected that irreverent man so deeply?

The dog only wagged her tail more wildly, then looked up into Kelly's face and grinned sweetly, as if love were the answer to everything.

DOWN BY THE moon-silvered shore, Zane took off his shirt, shook out his sleeping bag and climbed inside. He had his rifle beside him, and he lay facing the house so he could keep it in his line of vision. He watched her lit windows until they went dark.

Then he allowed himself to drift into an uneasy sleep; it was as if he were back in the jungles of Vietnam, ready to awaken at the least suspicious sound.

But for once, even as restlessly as he slept, he did not dream of those jungles or what he had seen in them.

He dreamed of a long-legged schoolteacher. She stood in the moonlight beside him and then began taking off her robe. Her beautiful, too-slender body gleamed in the pearly light and he looked at it a long time. Then he reached his hand up to her and drew her down beside him, opening the sleeping bag so she could slip in beside him.

Her long limbs were cool and silky against his, and her mouth was warm and silently eager for his.

But it was only a dream.

KELLY AWOKE to the sound of someone knocking insistently on the door.

Disoriented, not remembering where she was, she sat up in bed, looking about her a bit wildly. From the state of the twisted bed sheets, she'd obviously spent a restless night. A few stray beams of sunlight streamed through the slits of the bedroom's miniblinds and she could hear the muted songs of birds.

This wasn't her bedroom in her mother's house, it wasn't Cleveland and there was an odd little dog curled up at her feet. The dog looked at her guiltily, wagging her tail.

Kelly ran her hand over her tousled hair. Everything came back in a dizzying rush. The dog must have crept into her bed. And beneath her pillow was a bag of uncut jewels. Who was at the door? Zane? Zane had spent the night on the shore.

She leaped up, throwing on her robe and belting it tightly. When she swung the door open, she gave a sigh, partly of irritation, partly of relief. Zane stood there, a battered coffeepot in hand. He wore jeans, his riding boots and a red T-shirt that comfortably draped the complex contours of his muscles. He also wore a smug smile, one eyebrow raised.

"Madame's coffee," he said, holding the pot a bit higher.

"Oh, come in," she said in resignation, unlocking the screen door and swinging it open. The dog ran out, dancing about madly as if in celebration of a new morning.

"Did you really sleep out there all night?" Kelly asked.

"Earth was my pillow, heaven my canopy. All night long the lake, its face silvered by stars, hummed its water music. In short, yes. Slept fine."

He stepped to the table and set down the coffeepot. In his other hand he held a white paper bag, which he also put down. "Doughnuts," he said. "For milady. I brought them last night. I hope milady likes buttermilk."

Kelly crossed her arms and stared at him, her mouth sardonic. "Are you always this poetic in the morning?"

He raised an eyebrow. "Why? Are you implying you'd like to wake up next to a poetic man? Or an unpoetic one?"

She set her mouth more grimly, feeling her cheeks burn. "Don't talk like that. I know you only do it to embarrass me. Leave if you're going to talk that way."

He studied her with such intensity that her face burned more hotly. For a long moment the silence throbbed between them. "I pretty much talk the way I want," he said at last. "But I forget. You're the schoolteacher. Used to giving orders. Right, Miss Priss? I really *do* scare you, don't I? I think all men scare you."

"I'm not," she said with emphasis, "a *priss*. And you don't scare me. If you want a cup of coffee, pour it yourself. I'm going to get dressed."

She belted her robe more firmly, tossed her head and stalked back into the bedroom to get her clothes, trying to project an air of fearlessness. Then she went into the bathroom, shutting the door behind her and locking it with a loud click.

She gritted her teeth as she turned on the water to wash her face. How could he be so chivalric as to spend the night on the hard shore guarding her, how could he be so thoughtful as to bring her coffee and doughnuts, and at the same time be so utterly, maddeningly, completely irritating? Did it come naturally to him, or had he lain awake figuring out how to make her prickle with anger and embarrassment? What was he thinking now, the devil, as he sat out there?

SHE HAD *flounced* into the bathroom, Zane thought, smiling to himself. You didn't see many women these days who flounced well, especially tall ones. She was mistress of a lost art. He doubted if she'd ever been a mistress in any other sense. For all her pretended haughtiness, she truly didn't seem comfortable around a man.

Too bad, he mused, going to the cupboard and taking out mugs and plates. She woke up looking good, something else most women couldn't do. Her skin was rosy, the thick chestnut hair shining and tumbled, and she had such a dramatic bone structure she didn't have to rely on makeup in order to look striking.

As for her long body, hidden so adequately by the oversize robe, he could only rely on memory and imagination. He recalled how Jimmie had once affectionately described her: "She's just this coltish racehorse of a kid—legs go up to her neck." Well, the foal had grown into a tall, proud, restless filly, but her legs, he clearly recalled, still went on forever.

He sat and poured himself a mug of coffee, took a doughnut and bit into it thoughtfully. Long-legged, small-breasted, slender to a fault, she was built like a model. He didn't usually like that. He wasn't sure why he liked it on her.

If she had a different sort of personality, he might flirt with her in earnest, but she wasn't his type. She was too much of the old stereotype of a schoolteacher: prim, overly controlled, sexually inhibited, and besides that, she had terrible taste in literature.

He shrugged. Still, he'd had one hell of a dream about her. The memory of it still sent a slow burn through his blood.

He shouldn't tease the woman, he knew, if for no other reason than she was the niece of Jimmie, his friend. But she'd get that superior look on her face, and he'd remember what she'd done with Jimmie's books, and he couldn't resist. He, a man of considerable discipline, simply could not resist. It was as if she awoke some small, hot demon within him, complete with sharpened pitchfork.

The bathroom door opened and she emerged, the beautiful wild chestnut hair imprisoned in a short braid that fell just below her shoulders.

She hadn't bothered to put on makeup, which momentarily irritated his vanity. Didn't she think he was worth the effort to try to look her best? Then the demon in him smirked in satisfaction. Maybe she was afraid to look her best. She didn't want to invite any sort of sexual advance.

Unlike yesterday, she wore jeans instead of shorts, hiding her golden legs. Her red-and-white striped knit shirt was oversize, nearly disguising her subtle curves. Yes, she made sure she was covered up as much as was feasible on a summer day. So mentally, for his own amusement, he undressed her, assessed her and rated her, for the most part, favorably.

KELLY DIDN'T LIKE the look in those deep gray eyes, but she tried to ignore it. She sat down as primly as possible, poured herself a cup of coffee and took a doughnut. It occurred to her that she couldn't remember ever having breakfast with any man other than Jimmie. Occasionally she had had breakfast with boys in college, but that's all they had been— boys, not men.

There was nothing even slightly *boyish* about Zane. Perhaps that was what so perplexed Kelly. That and the paradox that for all his demonic traits, he was somehow attractive, blast him.

"Did you sleep well?" he asked, smiling over his cup. Somehow he made the question resonate with intimacy.

"Well enough," she said shortly. She realized she would sooner be trying to separate eight six-year-olds in a playground fight than sit across from this man again. How could she find him attractive? she asked herself crossly. Cissie would be appalled. Kelly was appalled herself. She bit into her doughnut with a vengeance.

"Fang guarded you well?"

"Oh, for heaven's sake," she muttered. "I can't call that silly thing 'Fang.' The word would stick in my throat."

"Then what'll you call her?"

She sipped the coffee, which she had to admit was excellent. "I don't know. 'Pollyanna,' maybe. Pollyanna's a character in a children's book. She never stopped being cheerful. Neither does the dog."

"Polly*anna?*" he asked in disbelief. "That's a terrible name for a dog. It's too long. Why don't you call her 'Happy' or 'Spot' or something?"

She narrowed her eyes at his criticism. "Spot? You don't have much imagination, do you?" It was an irritating thing to say, she realized. But, then, he was such a consistently irritating man that he brought it upon himself.

He gave her one of his long, silent, maddening stares. "No," he said, his mouth quirking down at one corner. "I guess I don't. So what do you plan to do with—can I bring myself to say it?—Pollyanna?"

Kelly's face went thoughtfully sad. "I don't know. I can't keep her. My mother's allergic to dogs. I'll have to give her away. All these animals, the cats, too. But I can't give them to the humane society. If nobody adopted them, they'd be—disposed of, and I couldn't stand that. Jimmie loved them."

He poured himself another cup of coffee. "I'm impressed. You do have a heart."

"Of *course* I have a heart!" Kelly said impatiently. She had a heart that was all too easily touched lately; that was her problem. "But it won't be easy finding homes for five full-grown cats and a manic dog."

Her face brightened slightly. She looked at Zane with thoughtful interest. "You," she said, almost smiling. "You could take the dog. And a cat or two. You live on a farm.

And Jimmie would *love* for a friend to have them. Maybe you could take *all* the cats.''

His expression went stonily blank. "Me? No, thanks. I have coon dogs. They'd have the cats for lunch. And as for the dog, a thousand times no. Anything that happy all the time would depress me."

"She's a very loving dog," Kelly said in Pollyanna's defense.

"Yes. She'd love a psychopath. She'd love an ax murderer. She'd love a ghoul. She has no discrimination. I do. And I discriminate against her."

Kelly sighed. She would have to take out a classified ad in the local newspapers. And she'd have to write an extremely eloquent ad for any results, a veritable masterpiece of an ad. She sank into depressed silence.

He interrupted her unhappy reverie with a blunt question. "Why do you still live with your mother?"

She looked up. He was staring at her again over the top of his coffee mug.

"There's plenty of room," she said with a careless shrug. "Where could I find a better place on my salary? And she can use the rent. And the company. We like each other's company."

"But neither of you much likes men, is that it?"

Kelly had been raising her doughnut to take another bite, but instead she set it back on her plate. "I beg your pardon," she said, her voice indignant. "That's a rather personal question."

He lifted one big shoulder in indifference. "I'm a personal person. I'm just asking. Jimmie said your mother was pretty well burned out on love. That your father soured her on men for good."

Kelly felt self-consciousness knotting painfully in her throat. Her father had been a big man, a handsome man and a charming one. But he had lied to Cissie and cheated on her, and when he'd finally betrayed her one time too many, Cissie, to survive, had hardened her heart against him and shut him out of their lives.

He had gone without protest, apparently happier without the shackles of wife and child. He had never sent Cissie a dime of child support; he'd drifted off to the West Coast, and he'd never tried to contact them. He'd never bothered to send so much as a Christmas card or a birthday card to Kelly.

He had died five years ago in Sacramento, California, and Cissie and Kelly hadn't even found out he was dead until a year later. When Kelly had learned of his death, she'd felt nothing. The girl who usually felt so much that she'd spent years learning to control her emotions had felt nothing at all.

Cissie had raised her single-handedly, and Kelly gave Cissie all the love she should feel for two parents, and all the loyalty, as well. If Zane was trying to criticize Cissie, she wouldn't allow it.

She drew herself up straighter in her chair. When she spoke, frost nipped her words. "My mother," she said from between her teeth, "went through living hell with my father. When he left us, he never looked back. Not once. He would have burned anyone out."

Her tone, the angry, imperious look on her face, should have made him flinch, even cringe. Instead he looked unimpressed, almost slightly bored. "So Jimmie said. But he felt bad that she shut herself off from any other relationships, that's all. He wished she'd found more happiness."

Kelly's blue eyes snapped fire. "My mother is quite happy, thank you. You've heard the saying, 'A woman needs a man the way a fish needs a bicycle'? Well, it's true. This may come as a shock to your masculine ego, but a woman does *not* need a man to be happy."

He smiled, condescension and scorn in the line of his mouth. "I didn't say she did," he said. "Your uncle worried about her, not me. But he may have had a point. So you live together, just the two of you, the librarian and the schoolteacher.''

Kelly's jaw clenched more tightly in defiance. He made them sound like two repressed spinsters, afraid of love and afraid of life. "Yes. The librarian and the schoolteacher. Does it bother you?"

He pushed his empty mug away. The muscles of his shoulders moved sinuously beneath his red shirt. "Very little bothers me. And you're going to be a writer, correct?" His voice practically dripped with mockery.

"I *am* a writer," she said haughtily. "I've published two books." Then, because that statement alone seemed grandiose, she added, "Maybe they didn't sell a million copies, and maybe I'm not famous, but I *am* a writer."

He pretended to be impressed. "My," he said, nodding. "Two books. My." He seemed to ponder this a moment. "May I ask you a question?"

She regarded him with suspicion. She was sure the question would be meddling or rude. "What?" she asked, her voice as cooly controlled as before.

True emotion showed in his rugged face, and the emotion was irritation. "What in *hell* do you write *about?*" he demanded.

"What do you mean?"

"Living that way, you and your mother, cutting yourself off from life and feeling, what do you write *about?* A writer has to be open to experience, not shut up like a clam."

"I do feel," Kelly said hotly. "I'm *not* shut off from life—I teach—I have twenty-five children in class who are a bigger dose of life and reality than most people experience. I see them laughing and crying and growing and hurting—"

She paused, wondering whether to rein in her anger at him. No, she thought, and let it gallop. "And who are *you* to judge me? To tell me what a writer should be? I haven't seen any evidence of your great literary ability. *You* even like Farley Collins."

"Of course I like Farley Collins," he snapped back. "I *am* Farley Collins, damn it."

What he said didn't register at first. "I wouldn't doubt it for a minute," she said angrily. "You're just the sort who would be. I wouldn't put it past you at all—"

Her face paled. She looked at the big man across from her as if seeing him for the first time. Her lips parted in unpleasant surprise and disbelief. Shock threatened to choke off her voice.

"I don't believe you," she managed to say. "If you were, Jimmie would have said so. He was always talking about those wretched—those books. He would have said if he'd known Farley Collins."

"He didn't *know* it," Zane ground out, and again he swore. "He knew I wrote, and when I didn't say much about it, he was gentleman enough not to ask. I don't usually tell people. Instead I tell them I make my money writing Westerns and I can't use my own name because it'd be confused with Zane Grey's. I don't tell them what name I write under at all because that's the way I like it. And I wouldn't have told you, except on the off chance it might knock some of the all-fired arrogance out of you. Ha!"

"I don't believe you," she repeated, staring at him as if hypnotized. And she didn't. She had always imagined Farley Collins as a pale, spidery gnome of a man with hunched shoulders, thin hair slicked back like Dracula's and wild eyes alit with insane fantasies. She had imagined he never went out into the sunlight and that he did weird things like sleep in a coffin. It had never occurred to her that Collins might be a large, healthy man who could fish or ride a horse or use a canoe or carry a rifle.

"I *am* Farley Collins," he retorted, his jaw every bit as stubborn as hers, "and I can prove it. I picked the name

Farley because of my favorite movie—*Strangers on a Train*. Do you know it?''

"Yes." She nodded numbly. "Alfred Hitchcock."

"Who played the lead?" he demanded.

She swallowed, feeling dazed. "Farley Granger."

His mouth twisted with even greater scorn. "My favorite mystery novel is *The Moonstone*. Do you know who wrote it—schoolteacher?"

She nodded again, feeling slightly sick. "Yes. Wilkie Collins."

"Okay," he said, and real anger glinted in his deep-set eyes. "Easy, right? Farley Collins. I've written twenty-two books, and the best one was *Her Demon Lover*. I took the title from a poem. Samuel Taylor Coleridge—'Kubla Khan.' Do you know *that?*"

"Yes," she said. Her voice sounded weak in her ears, not really her voice.

"So do I," he said with passion. "Coleridge described a spellbound place:

"A savage place! as holy and enchanted
As e'er beneath a waning moon was haunted
By woman wailing for her demon lover!"

He glowered at her, his upper lip turning up at one corner. "And if you still had a copy of the book, you could read his lines at the beginning."

She eyed him warily. "I do have a copy," she said without emotion. "I *will* see."

She rose and walked to the bedroom, took the copy of *Her Demon Lover* from the dresser and carried it back to the kitchen. She sat at the table, gave Zane another suspicious glance and opened the book. On the page preceding the first chapter were the exact lines he had quoted.

Stunned, she swallowed, once more feeling the knot of self-consciousness blocking her throat. She raised her eyes to meet his, which still had anger in their gray depths.

"Still don't believe me?" he asked, almost sneering. "Okay. Turn to the first chapter."

Grateful to escape making eye contact with him, she obeyed. She turned the page. Her eyes rested on the opening words.

As she read them, he recited them:

"That night Serena dreamed she stood in the orchard by moonlight, and the fallen apple blossoms lay so thickly in the grass that they looked like drifts of silver snow. Alma, the old gypsy woman claimed that demons lived in the orchard, and sometimes one could hear them laughing in the moonlight, far away as if the sound were carried on the wings of the night wind...."

He went on relentlessly, reciting the long opening paragraph word for word, pausing now and then to criticize a particular turn of phrase. "I should have said," he'd say, then amend the line, improving it. He plunged on, his voice righteous, until she slammed the book shut in frustration and forced herself to look at him again.

Her face blazed with embarrassment. "All right. I believe you. Why didn't you tell me from the start? I wouldn't have said all those—those things."

He narrowed his eyes cynically. "Because I hardly ever tell anybody. I like my privacy. Besides, what difference does it make if you said it if that's what you think? You think what I write stinks, so why be a hypocrite?"

"I—I—" stammered Kelly, but she could think of nothing to say. She remembered how ruthlessly she had criticized his work, how she had even kicked one of his books as it lay in the grass. She winced. How would she have felt if she'd seen someone treat one of her books in such a man-

ner? Then, to add insult to injury, she had given all the
novels to the thrift store, as if they were not good enough to
be in the same house with her.

"I'm sorry," she said miserably. It was not an original
apology; it was not adequate. But it was the only one that
came to her.

"Don't be," he said, standing.

When he stood, he seemed to loom, to take up too much
room in the small kitchen area. Kelly stood, too, if only so
she would not feel so dwarfed by him. He was leaving; she
had offended him deeply, and she had done so out of igno-
rance. Why, she thought, humiliated, hadn't she kept her
opinions to herself?

Yet part of her mind argued that her opinions were at
least sincere. She hated the sort of work this man did. She
just shouldn't have said so with such venom.

"What you *might* do," he muttered, reaching for the
book and taking it, "is read this thing." He shook it for
emphasis. "I don't mind criticism. I don't even mind harsh
criticism. What I do mind is cheap shots from people who
haven't read me at all. Know what you're talking about before you shoot your mouth off."

He thrust the book back into her hands and she flinched
as she took it. "Listen," she said, trying to regain her com-
posure, "it's just a question of taste, that's all. Mine isn't the
same as yours. I don't like horror because I think there are
enough horrible things in the world. And I don't see the
point of scaring people—"

"And I told you," he said, bending nearer, his lip curling in defiance. "I like scaring people. I'm good at it. Damn
good, in fact."

She blinked up at him, her emotions in a confusing swirl.
She shouldn't worry about damaging his ego, she thought.
It was undamageable. It was huge and hard as granite. It
was a Gibraltar of an ego. She turned her face away, her
embarrassment mingling with fresh anger.

"You don't frighten me," she said passionately. But she didn't dare meet his mocking gaze.

"Don't I?" he asked, his voice dangerously soft. "Then allow me to try again. Because it's easy to see what scares you most. It's child's play. The simplest, most basic thing in the world scares you."

He reached out and grasped her upper arms.

Kelly gasped at his touch and at the intensity of his voice. Reluctantly she raised her eyes to his again, and she was surprised to see wicked glee flickering in his gaze.

He pulled her to him and bent so that his face drew nearer to hers. "Brace yourself, Miss Cordiner," he warned in a silky whisper. "You're about to be terrified. By an expert."

Then he took her in his arms, stared into her eyes and smiled a slow, taunting smile. He looked at her for a long moment. Kelly gazed back, her heart beating against her ribs like an imprisoned bird. She felt paralyzed, hypnotized. When she didn't resist, he drew her closer still, and his smile faded. The laughter fled from his eyes.

He lowered his face to hers and kissed her with a ferocity that would have been, in truth, terrifying had it not also been so achingly sweet.

CHAPTER FOUR

FOR A MOMENT Kelly tried to struggle, but for a moment only. She was indeed frightened, but not by Zane's over-powering strength or the way his lips had hotly comman-deered hers.

What truly frightened her was that the touch of his lips awoke a wild, exquisite emotion in her that swept through her body like a flash flood, drowning any real protest.

His arms had captured her inexorably, wrapping around her to press her body against his. She felt the strength of his thighs as they strained against her own, and the hot width of his hard chest pushed against her breasts.

For more than a week, ever since Jimmie's death, she had felt saddened, confused and tired from too many demands on her. She had fallen asleep last night feeling wearied and weakened by life's complexities. Now she was surrounded by strength and a titillating energy, swept up in a dark power that made everything seem simple and vital again.

Warm and slightly dazed, she wanted to give herself to that strength and darkness, let it carry her on to some scarcely imaginable island of pleasure and revivifying magic. She did not feel so much as if his body were robbing hers as somehow promising to reward and restore it.

Yet she knew his lips were committing a slow, sure pi-racy, energetic yet languid at the same time. He kissed her with such masterly thoroughness that her mind seemed to swim through a blackness shot through with dazzles of gold.

His jaw, stubborn, hard and unshaven, grated against her softer one. His mouth, firm and hot, opened, and so did hers beneath its persuasions.

His tongue, like a silky flame, skimmed over her lips, then stroked her tongue, which stammered against his as if trying to learn this new language.

Oh, it was pleasant, Kelly thought, to be held firmly by such strong arms, to be warmed by such a wealth of power, to be kissed with such ardor that the rest of the world faded to near nothingness.

Kelly, don't! It was her mother's voice, almost as clear as if Cissie were in the room. Suddenly Kelly knew what she was doing was both dangerous and foolish. This, the narcotic pleasure of a man's expert touch, was the poison that had nearly ruined Cissie's life and tainted Kelly's since childhood.

"Kelly, be careful of *that* trap," her mother had always said of sex and love. Kelly remembered the haunted, shamed look in Cissie's eyes when she'd spoken of such things, the unhappy slant of her mouth, the air of hurt and resentment. Love had done that to Cissie. Love and the drugging lure of sex.

It was then, because Zane's lips felt both so right and wrong upon her own, that Kelly was truly frightened. Her mind skittered off some high abyss, falling into the pit of shadowy terrors that had haunted her most of her life.

Part of her wanted to flee Zane; part wanted to stay, fighting him and punishing him for awakening emotions that were both too many and too powerful to be faced. Reality seemed to dim and sway about her. Then it solidified, hard, cold and without illusion.

Her lips grew unresponsive beneath his seeking ones; her body turned awkwardly stiff and cold. Raising her hands to his chest, she pushed away and twisted her face from his.

He drew back only slightly, as if her push had been nothing but a tap to divert his attention. His lips were only inches from her ear, and she could feel the warmth of his breath when he spoke. His voice was low.

"Frightened?"

"No," she answered, struggling to escape his embrace, "repulsed. Let go of me, you—you sadist."

He merely held her more tightly, until she realized escape was impossible until he permitted it. "You don't kiss me as if you're repulsed."

"I didn't kiss you at all," she almost hissed. "Let go of me. I—I'll sue you. I'll smear your name all over the papers. This is sexual harassment. This is—"

He laughed. "Ah, Kelly, I'm impressed. The perfect argument to turn any respectable man's blood cold. And I am a respectable man, I assure you. A sadist? Never. A sadist takes pleasure in someone else's pain. I don't. I take pleasure only in other's pleasure. Harassment? No. Unless trying to give pleasure is harassment."

She could not resist giving his chest another shove, ineffectual as it might be. "Let go of me, you son of a—"

He cut her off, gripping her shoulders and turning her face so she had to look up at him. "Don't say anything you'll regret, Priss. Don't worry. I wouldn't force you to do anything you don't want to. Except, perhaps, make you face the truth—that everyone in the world is afraid of something. And you, so civilized, so self-contained, are afraid of raw emotion—of any emotion beyond a certain, safe little circle. Jimmie was always worried you would be."

The tone of his voice, the strange set of his smile, both tender and contemptuous, lessened her fear but not her anger. By some strange, deep instinct, she knew he wouldn't hurt her; it was against his nature. But she had irritated and insulted him, and he intended to teach her a lesson. He had wanted to teach it in the most effective and humiliating way.

"Get out of here," she ordered, her heart drumming insanely. "What my uncle ever saw in you—why he ever had you for a friend—"

He laid his forefinger against her lips, silencing her. "You'll never believe it, kid, but in some ways we were two of a kind. We were a lot alike, Jimmie and I."

Kelly gave a bitter laugh and shook away his hand from her face. "You're nothing alike. I don't know how he could ever trust you—"

His smile grew harder, more ironic. "He trusted me because he knew he could."

He was holding her only by one shoulder now, and not very firmly, but he kept his face close to hers. She should have wrenched out of his grasp, stepped away, but for some reason, she did not. The reason, she told herself, was pride.

She stared up into his gray eyes, trying to shame or intimidate him, force him to be the one to back away. He would not. She realized, with another frisson of uneasiness, that if she looked into those eyes long enough, it would be possible to become lost in them. He had the sort of irises she always thought of as cracked glass. The color was deep, but not clear, webbed as if by shatter marks.

All sorts of complexities lived behind those eyes, all sorts of contradictions, all sorts of emotions. At the moment, to her surprise, she thought she saw regret in them, and something almost akin to sorrow.

He frowned. "I'm sorry," he said simply. It was the most unexpected thing he could have said. But she understood that what he said was true. He *was* sorry.

"I'll even break my own rule and say it twice."

He raised his hand and touched her face lightly, his hand lingering on her jaw so lightly that her flesh tingled.

"I'm sorry. But you made me as mad as any woman has ever made me in my life."

The regret in his gaze died away and something else appeared, dark and less readable. He toyed with a strand of her hair that had come loose, curling it around his finger. "Almost from the first time I saw you, I wanted to kiss you. Yet I didn't want to. Not at all."

Kelly took a deep breath, so sharp it stabbed her chest.
She wondered, confusedly, if he was about to kiss her again.
If he tried, would she again find herself letting him? Her lips
parted slightly and she couldn't take her gaze from the
complicated crystal depths of his eyes.

"Don't be frightened of me, Kelly," he said softly. "You
don't have to be."

Instead of drawing nearer, he stepped away. His hands left
her face and shoulder. He moved to the table, then turned
to look at her.

"I could never bring myself to hurt—intentionally hurt—
anything that Jimmie loved. But unintentionally—out of
anger or pride, people sometimes do things to each other.
Anger and pride aren't admirable qualities, but we seem to
bring them out in each other. It's unfortunate."

She said nothing, only stood watching him warily, all her
senses supernaturally alert.

A stolid blankness settled over his face. "So let's declare
a truce. You don't insult my writing, and I won't insult
yours—or your life-style. If Jimmie had ever seen us like
that, he'd have been so depressed he'd have gone off drunk
for a month. I'll be back. I told you, I know where his ashes
are supposed to go. I have business today, but I can take you
there tomorrow evening."

Still she said nothing.

He lifted the coffeepot from the table and held it toward
her in a sort of mock salute. "From here on out, let's keep
our criticism of each other objective, not personal, all
right?"

She took another deep breath. "I thought you were a
personal person."

He smiled, but there was no humor in it. "I am. But I
think in your case, I'll make an exception. Take care. And
get those jewels to the bank."

He turned and walked out the door. As he did so, the
brown-and-white dog darted in, running so hard that she

skidded on the linoleum and nearly crashed into the table leg. This delighted her so much that she began to do a frantic hornpipe around Kelly, her claws chattering on the floor.

Kelly hardly noticed. Her hand raised unconsciously to her lips, she stepped toward the window. She watched Zane, his wide back, narrow hips, stride toward the shore. His camping gear lay in a neat pile, the remnants of a small fire smoldering among the pebbles, and the canoe was upside down beneath the trees.

Her lips still throbbed from his kisses; her pulses still hammered from the power of his embrace.

She watched as with a few economical movements he doused the remains of the fire, packed up his equipment, righted the canoe and dragged it to the water. He loaded it and got in, setting off as surely and swiftly as some wild creature born to the cliff-lined lake.

She watched, broodingly, until he disappeared around the edge of the cove. With a start, she realized she still had her fingertips pressed to her mouth. She drew them away, folding her arms self-consciously. She felt as stunned as if she'd been knocked unconscious and hadn't quite come to completely. She shook her head, but it didn't help. She still felt dazed.

Troubled, she remembered Zane's kisses. Unwanted, uninvited, ungentlemanly, they had nevertheless done exactly what he had said: they had both terrified her and given her pleasure. They terrified her precisely *because* they gave her pleasure.

He said he would return. She had flung the statement back in his face, telling him to stay away. But somehow, deep within, she recognized the forbidden truth. She wanted him to come back.

Every time she saw him, he turned her world upside down; yet against all reason, she wanted him to return. He would, she knew.

What then?

ALL DAY Kelly struggled to thrust Zane from her mind, to focus on the business at hand and nothing else. She gave Jimmie's little house a superficial cleaning, changed into one of the few dresses she had brought, a short-sleeved blue chambray, and drove to Fayetteville to see Phoebe Carrington, Jimmie's lawyer.

Phoebe Carrington was a small, wiry middle-aged woman with crackling brown eyes and a no-nonsense air. Briskly she told Kelly what had to be done and how. She herself would take care of filing the will. The tedious paperwork and legal details might take as long as six months to complete, but she would get a special order so Kelly could put the house and all other goods up for sale as soon as possible.

Kelly didn't mention the jewels. Jimmie had kept the stones a secret all these years and some cautious inner impulse told her to do the same.

After leaving the lawyer's she went to Henion's, a jewelry store on the town square. Mr. Henion was so old that his skin looked like the thinnest of parchment, and his gnarled hands trembled slightly when he took the stones she showed him. But his eyes, a light, bright blue, still shone with an intelligence that age had not dulled.

One by one he stared at the rough stones through his jeweler's loupe. Then he looked at Kelly, his pale eyes piercingly serious. "Young lady," he said, "you have some extremely valuable stones here. Be careful. Be very careful."

Kelly felt a frisson of fear ripple through her. *Be careful with these jewels,* she thought. *And be careful of the man that held them for you.*

Both nervous and excited, she went to the nearest bank, rented a safety deposit box and locked the jewels securely away. Then she went to one of the city's modest shopping centers and found a phone booth. She gave the operator her credit card number and called her mother.

Cissie was disbelieving and aghast when Kelly told her about the gems.

"He left $300,000 worth of jewels sitting in his house?" Cissie almost yelped. "Where did he get them? How did he get them? How do you know they're real? Anybody could fool Jimmie. He was too trusting. He left them just *sitting* in that house? Why, anybody could have walked in and taken them. They can't be real."

Cissie's thoughts were leaping back and forth like a confused grasshopper, and Kelly took a deep breath, trying to be the calm one. "They're real," Kelly said. "I had a jeweler look at them. And Jimmie didn't leave them in the house. He had a neighbor keep them."

"A *neighbor?*" Cissie cried. "A person doesn't just hand over something worth $300,000 to a neighbor! Who is this neighbor—is it somebody trying to—to pull a scam on us? Don't trust this person! Who has these—these things now? *What* in heaven's name is going on?"

Kelly squared her shoulders. The less she told Cissie about Zane the better, but her mother's words about him filled her with guilt and anxiety. "Don't trust this person," she'd said.

"I've got the jewels," Kelly said. "I put them in a safety deposit box in the bank."

"I don't trust banks," Cissie objected. "My grandfather lost all his money in the depression when the banks failed. I don't like this, Kelly. I don't like any of it. And who, please, is this neighbor?"

"There's no place in the world safer than a safety deposit box," Kelly explained, trying to keep the conversation away from Zane. "I signed a card and have a key. To get into the box, I have to sign a form so they can check my signature against the one they have on file. Then they escort me into the vault. The box won't open without *both* their key and mine—it's a foolproof system. Nobody else can get in."

"What if you lose the key?" Cissie challenged. "And what about this neighbor? You're being very evasive. Is it a man? Jimmie talked about some man down there. I don't want you taking up with some strange man. He could be after the money."

Kelly gritted her teeth. The last thing Zane needed was her money. No, he threatened something far more personal than her wealth.

"Listen, Mother," she said, "the bank said I should have you cosign for the box in case of emergency. I'm sending you a form to sign and mail back so that they have your signature on file, too. And I've got a key for you, too. I'll send it with the form."

"How do you know this neighbor isn't a jewel thief or a smuggler or something worse," Cissie asked, "trying to get us to handle this—this stuff for him? Or maybe he'll get in that box and switch things around—you don't know."

Kelly shook her head and ran her hand through her hair. "Mother, *nobody* can get into the box except you or me. It's impossible. Only *our* signatures and *our* keys allow anybody to get into it. Settle down. You should leave those sorts of ideas to the police shows on television."

"The police shows are a scandal and an outrage," Cissie said haughtily, "and I'm proud not to watch them. They're violent and cheap. People should be reading worthwhile books, not watching police shows. But I wasn't born yesterday. I *am* aware that there are unscrupulous people in the world."

Yes, Kelly thought hopelessly. *You know because you were married to one. And I know because he was my father. Trust doesn't come easy in our family.*

"Mother," she said, marshaling her patience, "Relax. I mean it. The jewels are real, they're safe and it's absolutely impossible for anyone but you or me to get to them. The bank says nobody's ever gotten into one illegally. Ever. It can't be done."

"Well, don't you trust that neighbor," Cissie said. "I don't like the sound of him. Or is it a her? I never told you, but Jimmie was taken in more than once by a woman. He never had an ounce of sense when it came to the opposite sex."

Kelly swallowed hard. "The neighbor is a he," she said. She did not add that he was a tall, rather handsome, wealthy and highly perplexing he.

"Don't trust him, just don't trust him," Cissie said flatly, then abruptly changed the subject. "What about your writing? Don't get caught up in some wild goose chase. You went down there to write, not just take care of Jimmie's business. Be sure to take time for yourself, Kelly."

Kelly tried to assure her that everything was fine, but when she remembered Zane's deep-set, mocking eyes, the touch of his hands and the taste of his lips, she felt anything but fine. She felt uneasy and vulnerable.

"Be careful," Cissie kept saying. "Be careful, Kelly, be careful, be careful."

WHEN KELLY RETURNED to Jimmie's house, she was unpleasantly surprised to see another car parked among the pines. A dented and dusty blue compact sat by the smallest of the houses that neighbored Jimmie's. It was a little brown house no larger than a garage, and Kelly had noticed the For Rent sign in front of it.

Apparently the new dweller had heard the sound of Jimmie's Jeep, for the back door of the house swung open and a small, pleasantly plump woman with curly white hair and a motherly face appeared, smiling widely. She gave a cheerful wave of her right hand. Her left hand clutched the head of a wooden cane.

The woman's smile faded when she saw Kelly at the wheel. At first she looked puzzled; then a light of recognition seemed to cross her face. As Kelly parked the Jeep and got out, the woman hobbled toward her. She was somewhere between fifty-five and sixty-five, and her left leg was in a white cast.

"Hello," the woman said, cocking her head and examining Kelly closely. "I'll bet you're Jimmie's niece, aren't you? You surely do have his blue eyes and wavy hair."

Kelly nodded, unsure of herself. She was a city person and suspicious of the gregariousness of strangers. The woman had a sugary voice that didn't quite match her plain, open face.

"Jim and I were neighbors last year," the woman said, with a friendly smile. "He just talked and talked about you. You and your mama both—Cissie, isn't it? And you're—Cathy, isn't that right?"

"Kelly," Kelly corrected, trying to be polite and to take the woman's measure at the same time. "Kelly Cordiner."

"Of course," the woman said with a bubbling, jolly laugh. "Kelly. How could I forget? Jimmie's little writer. He's so proud of you. Are you still writing?"

"I'm still trying," Kelly replied, nonplussed. This couldn't be one of Jimmie's notorious women, she told herself. The woman must be twenty years older than Jimmie, as plump and homey as a fresh-baked biscuit. She seemed to know him well and be genuinely interested in his family.

"Well, *good,*" said the woman warmly, ignoring Kelly's hesitation. "I'm Mrs. Mavis Pruer." She thrust out her hand.

Kelly offered hers in return and Mavis Pruer pumped it heartily. Mavis was an ordinary-looking woman, but she was carefully groomed, and her bright, quick eyes seemed to miss no detail. She wore a modest red knit top and her starched white shorts came nearly to her knees.

She kept her left hand curled around the curved handle of her wooden cane, and on her left leg the cast extended from ankle to knee.

Mavis caught the flicker of Kelly's curious glance and released her hand. She made a dismissive gesture toward the
cast. "Cracked my car up," she said ruefully. "Broke my
leg. But that wasn't going to keep me away from my two
weeks at the lake. I couldn't live without my time at the lake.
No, ma'am. I'm just like Jimmie. I *love* this lake."

"Oh," Kelly said awkwardly. She hadn't meant for Mavis to catch her glancing at the cast, and the mention of
Jimmie filled her with foreboding. She hated to be the mes-
senger of bad news, but knew she must.

"And how *is* Jimmie?" Mavis asked with a wide smile.
"That scamp? Where is he? Out fishing?"

When Kelly broke the news as gently as she could, she was
dismayed by the stare of shocked disbelief that Mavis Pruer
gave her. The woman stared at her, eyes wide, for almost a
full minute. She said nothing and neither could Kelly.

Then Mavis further alarmed Kelly by bursting into tears.
The woman did not merely cry; she wept and sobbed. For a
moment she seemed incoherent with grief.

Oh, dear, Kelly thought, taken aback. She was used to
seeing children cry, but not adults. "There, there," she said
uneasily, and gave Mavis's shoulder an inept pat.

Mavis responded by hobbling forward a step, throwing
herself into Kelly's arms, laying her face against Kelly's
shoulder and sobbing even harder. Alarmed, Kelly felt the
woman's hot tears soaking through the blue cloth of her
dress.

"I adored that man," Mavis wept, choking out the words,
"I just *loved* him. He was the kindest, gentlest—" she dissolved into sobs again and clutched Kelly more tightly.

Oh, dear, thought Kelly, dismayed. "I—I," she stumbled, "I—Mrs. Pruer, don't feel bad. It happened very
quickly and he didn't suffer. He died in his sleep at my
mother's house. If he had to go, at least he had a merciful
death."

Mavis Pruer wailed more loudly. "That poor, unfortunate man," she managed to quaver at last. "Such a hard life—and then—his problem. The drinking. Oh, I knew better than to try to talk him out of it. My daddy had a drinking problem. You can't talk anybody into quitting. He has to *want* to quit. He couldn't help having the disease. I just prayed he'd decide to cure it."

Well, Kelly thought dismally, Mavis Pruer might be overly emotional, but at least she was compassionate. She patted the woman's back in a ginger motion.

"I swear, I'm so shocked my knees are weak. Would you walk me back to my place, honey?" Mavis released Kelly, dug into her pocket and drew out a sheaf of tissues. She tried to dry her streaming eyes and blew her nose, honking loudly. The hand holding her cane trembled slightly. She seemed almost undone by the shock.

"Of course," Kelly said, taking the woman's free arm to help support her.

"Do come in," Mavis said, catching hold of Kelly's hand when they reached her porch. "Please have a little glass of something with me and talk to me. Oh, this is *such* a blow."

Deftly she drew Kelly inside the house, which smelled musty. Dust specks floated in the sunlight that streamed through the windows.

"Sit, sit, sit," Mavis ordered distractedly. "I'll pour some lemonade. Please excuse the appearance. I only just moved in this afternoon—haven't dusted or *anything*. Oh, Jimmie gone—I just can't believe it."

She limped into the kitchen area, blowing her nose again. Then, seeming to gain control of herself, she went to the refrigerator and withdrew a quart bottle of lemonade. She poured two glasses, her hand still shaking.

Kelly went to help her carry the glasses. The little house was really just one long room, with the kitchen area at one end, flanked by a door that probably led to the bathroom.

Kelly carried the glasses to the coffee table that sat before the bulky couch, and made Mavis sit. Then she herself sat, holding the cold glass in her hand.

"You'll have to excuse me, honey," Mavis said, dabbing the last of the tears from her eyes. "I've always been emotional. My late husband used to say to me, 'Mavis you're too tenderhearted. You're too easily touched.' Well, I do apologize."

"Don't apologize," Kelly said, but in truth she hoped the woman wouldn't break into another torrent of tears.

"When did it happen?" Mavis asked, lifting her chin bravely.

"Just a little over a week ago," Kelly said. "My mother and I decided I should be the one to come down and take care of his things."

"He loved you both *so* much," Mavis said, her voice choked. "And he was *so* proud of your writing. What were the names of your books?"

"*The Lost Teddybear* and *My Pet Unicorn*," Kelly said. She sat stiffly, concerned to see fresh tears starting to glint in Mavis Pruer's eyes.

"Such lovely books," Mavis managed to say. "He insisted on reading them out loud to me. Just *lovely* books. So sweet and soothing. Just the thing to put a child to sleep."

"Thank you." Kelly was not sure she was pleased to be told her work could put readers to sleep. Squaring her shoulders, she took a long drink of lemonade. She suddenly yearned for the quiet and privacy of Jimmie's house.

"He wanted, more than anything in the world, to help you with your wonderful career," Mavis said with a bereaved sniff. "And to do something for your lovely mother. He said she'd had a hard life. Such an unfortunate marriage. Your father just—left you both behind, didn't he? Jimmie said it had been so hard on you both."

Kelly's spine stiffened more rigidly. She and Cissie were private people. She wished Jimmie hadn't discussed their affairs so freely. She nodded and tried to smile as if the memory of her father didn't hurt her, but the smile was forced, tight.

"Well," Mavis said with a philosophical shrug, "at least Jimmy provided for you. He wanted to make up for how your father treated you. He told me about his will. That everything went to the two of you. Yes, I'm sure that wherever he is, that makes him happy, that he can help you."

Kelly forced herself to smile and nod again, but said nothing.

"You've seen the will, of course?" Mavis asked, scrubbing at her eyes again with the crumpled tissues. "His lawyer had a copy. A Miss Carrington or Farrington in Fayetteville. You do know about the will, don't you?"

"Carrington," Kelly said, surprised again at how much Jimmie had confided in this woman. "Yes. I've seen it."

Mavis sighed deeply. "He had—something special for you—something valuable. Did you know that? A secret? Put away? Have you got it? Is it in a safe place?"

Kelly blinked, uncertain what to say. Jimmie must have trusted Mavis enough to tell her about the jewels. "Yes," she said, feeling evasive. "I took—everything to the bank this morning. To a safety deposit box. It's—fine."

Mavis seemed to think a long, solemn thought. "Good. He was a good man." She shook her head in sorrow. "But people took advantage of him. Especially women. What a shame. We all watched out for him the best we could. But— ugh! You should have seen some of those creatures he took up with." She shuddered daintily.

Kelly stared down into her lemonade. Jimmie's sexual peccadilloes seemed all too well known. "We?" she asked, crooking one eyebrow.

"Everyone who stays out here," Mavis said. "Some come on weekends and some for a few weeks at a time. The people who own the other houses. And people like me, who rent them. Oh, more will be coming along all summer."

Kelly's heart sank. Although she had found the isolation of Jimmie's house disconcerting, she had already come to like the quiet, the solitude.

"Yes," Mavis mused, her tear-stained face almost dreamy. "But I won't join much of the fun this year. I can barely get around with this leg. No hikes or swimming for me. But at least I can sit in the quiet and watch the birds. I do love our little birdie friends."

Kelly nodded politely. With elaborate casualness, she asked, "Do you know any of the other neighbors along the lake? I met one who'd been feeding Jimmie's dog and cats. A man named Zane Graye. He—helped me with the will and things."

"Graye?" Mavis gave a slight start, then a sniff of distaste. "No." She was silent a moment, as if deciding how much she should say. "I never met him. But, frankly, I've heard of him. Jimmie told me all about *him*. I don't think Jim would want you accepting help from *him*. He's got a reputation."

A weird prickle ran through Kelly's nerve ends. "Reputation?"

"A real Don Juan, if you know what I mean," Mavis said archly. "A pretty young girl like you should be on your guard. Don't get me wrong—Jimmie *liked* the man in a way. But he didn't approve of how he treated women. I guess his attitude is the more the merrier. And it's not out of loneliness, the way it was with Jimmie. It's just that certain men—you know—have a sort of devil in them."

Devil, Kelly thought, cold spreading through her. *Demon. Her Demon Lover.*

"And you've let him 'help' you." Mavis asked.

"Yes," Kelly said, feeling suddenly guilty.

Mavis studied her soberly, then pointed a finger at her, making a stabbing motion. "Maybe I shouldn't say this— but I think Jimmie would want me to. Watch out for that one. Be extremely careful."

"I intend to be," Kelly said, trying to keep her voice light and casual.

"I mean—" Mavis went on "—I could tell you tales about that man, honey. He sounds just like the way Jimmy described your father—no sense of responsibility. He's got more than one woods colt running around these parts."

"Woods colt?" Kelly had never heard the term. It conjured images of an elfin little horse in a magical forest.

"Il-le-gi-ti-mate chil-dren," Mavis said carefully, as if it were improper to utter words of such scandalous import in a casual tone.

Kelly felt a chill surge through her as powerfully as an electric shock. Illegitimate children? The musty little house seemed to clamp down around her, smothering her. Quickly, numbly, she drained her glass and set it on the table.

"I think I'd better be going," she said, smiling as best she could. "Thank you for the drink. Don't bother getting up. I'll see myself to the door."

"Any time," said Mavis, smiling in a way that made her bright little eyes twinkle, in spite of her tear-stained cheeks.

Kelly left, her heart hammering a hard, staccato rhythm in her chest. Zane had illegitimate children? Kelly hated nothing as much as a man who would abandon a child. With a quiver of revulsion, she thought of her own father. Zane was like him. No, perhaps he was even worse.

She thought of the fatherless children she'd had in her classes, their special problems and pain. She'd understood those problems, that pain, all too thoroughly. What she didn't understand was how men could do such things to innocent children. And, like a crazy woman, she had allowed herself to be attracted to him—insane!

She let herself into Jimmie's house and went into the bedroom. She felt a strange compulsion to get out of the blue dress as quickly as possible. Its shoulder was still damp with Mavis Pruer's tears.

She slipped out of it gratefully and stood half-naked, trying to decide what, in her limited wardrobe, to wear.

Her eyes fell on the thick book she had placed on the dresser. Its black cover seemed to stare back at her, as if in reproach or warning.

Her Demon Lover, the familiar title said. The silver words glinted against the blackness as if they had a life of their own.

Uneasily she remembered what everyone had told her today. *Be careful, be careful, be careful.*

CHAPTER FIVE

KELLY CHANGED back into her shorts and a T-shirt and set about cleaning Jimmie's place with a vengeance, mopping, washing, scrubbing. No matter how hard she worked, however, through her head ran a litany of disquieting words: *be careful, don't trust, watch out, woods colt.*

Woods colt. Had Zane really fathered an illegitimate child—or children? Mrs. Pruer claimed that he was no better than a Don Juan, and why would she lie? Kelly remembered how Zane had kissed her until her will had almost dissolved into acquiescence, sweet and warm. Wasn't that what a seducer did, overwhelm a woman with sensual desire?

And Zane was rich and, in a roundabout way, famous. Wasn't that how many male celebrities acted these days? They fathered children but made no commitments to the women who bore them. They were determined to seize it all, women, children, wealth, power, freedom. In return they gave nothing but the temporary intoxicating pleasure of their company. Kelly almost shuddered with disgust.

Don't think about him, she warned herself. *Put him out of your mind. Cissie's right about men. She always has been.*

The sun was starting to set, its slanting golden light making all the day's colors deeper and richer. Kelly sighed as she stared out at the lake. Zane said he would come this evening to take her to scatter Jimmie's ashes. Even though the prospect made her nervous, she must get ready, change her clothes. But she would be careful of him, just as everyone had warned.

When she heard his knock on the door, her heart flew up and lodged in her throat, and her breathing became shallow, like that of someone hiding and poised for flight.

She forced herself to take three deep breaths, then marched to the door. Standing as erect as she could, she flung it open majestically, as if she were a princess granting audience to a peasant.

When she saw him, her heart wedged itself in her throat more tightly. Zane was so tall and broad of shoulder he almost blocked her view of the pines and oaks behind him. The setting sun enriched his brown hair with gold, gilded his strong features.

He was so handsome, she thought with a sick, almost dizzy feeling, so dangerously, seductively handsome. Not like her father, whose pictures she had seen. Her father had been something of a pretty boy. But there was no prettiness in Zane, only an appearance of strength. And he used that appearance, she reminded herself, to prey on the weakness of others. Women's weaknesses.

"Yes?" she said, her chin held high.

"Yes, indeed," he said, looking her up and down through the screen door.

The dog capered, gleeful at his arrival, but Kelly ignored it and so did Zane.

GOOD LORD, but the woman looked beautiful in her strange, unique way, he thought. He felt a tightening in his chest and groin, a tremor of excitement quickening his blood. She had dressed just right, not formally, but with a natural, casual prettiness.

Her long legs and lean hips were hugged by jeans still new enough to be almost midnight blue, and she wore a sleeveless white camisole top trimmed with simple lace. It outlined her small, upthrust breasts, the narrow sleekness of her waist. Her sandals were white, and she had tied her wealth of chestnut hair back with a wide white ribbon.

Long body, long smooth arms and deliciously long legs, she gave the first impression of being almost as lean as a boy. But he remembered holding her, and she had felt soft, warm, curving and feminine in his arms. The high cheekbones, firm jaw and steady eyes gave her face an almost royal elegance.

Against his will, he had thought of her all day long. He'd done a damn fool thing, forcing his kiss on her like that. In the first place it was unlike him, and in the second, he'd never before found himself taking a woman's kiss by aggression. Women had always granted him all he wanted, and often, alas, more. His memory was jammed to overflowing with available women, eager and often overeager, beckoning to him, reaching for him, clutching at him.

It both piqued and intrigued him that this one didn't. When he had taken her in his arms and robbed her of those kisses, she had initially resisted, then responded with a naturalness and warmth that stormed his senses like a hurricane.

It was then that he had understood that she was ready for love, hungry for it, but didn't even know it. How does a man treat a woman in such a case? Respect such innocence and retreat from her? Or teach her all that physical love can be?

He looked at the way the afternoon light glinted in the glossy brown of her hair, the way her blue eyes met his with such wary steadiness. He kept his mouth clamped in a firm, expressionless line. Once more he allowed his eyes to travel slowly down, then up her tall body, from the gleam of her hair to her slim, half-naked feet and back again.

The only makeup she wore was a touch of pale lipstick, and that was all she needed. It made her full lips glisten against the tawny gold of her complexion.

Steady, he reminded himself with bemusement. At all times he must remember two things clearly. First, this was his friend's niece, and out of respect to Jim, he should keep his distance. Second, she didn't like him, and if truth be told, he didn't much like her, either. They had nothing in common.

She was a city woman, but oddly innocent in a mule-headed way. He was a cynical man of the rivers and lakes and woods, and he made his living exploring the dark side of the imagination, the side she hated.

No, he told himself. Stay away from her. She was designed to cause him nothing but trouble.

KELLY STARED UP at Zane for what seemed an endless moment. His mouth was so straight it seemed grim, and once more she found herself puzzled by the shifting expressions in the deep, webbed gray of his eyes. For a moment something akin to mockery seemed to hover there, then flick away to be replaced by a look more dangerous and hungry. Then that fleeting look dissolved into a thoughtful seriousness—that was just as quickly transformed back into mockery.

He wore tight, faded jeans pressed to a sharp crease, a leather belt with a silver buckle shaped like a wolf's head, and a long-sleeved blue-gray shirt, the collar open and the sleeves rolled up to his elbows.

A breeze had arisen, cooling the warm afternoon, and it fluttered his straight brown hair. Kelly's stomach fluttered, too.

For the hundredth time, she reminded herself to be careful, as she had been careful all her life. *Woods colt,* her brain whispered, as if the words were a strange charm to protect her. He was like her father, a man who didn't care. *Woods colt.* A woman might want such a man. That was natural, she thought with a surge of yearning. But she should never trust him.

"Are you ready?" he asked curtly, his lips hardly moving.

"Almost," she said, and turned from the door. She didn't ask him in, although she knew it was rude not to. She felt safer with a barrier, even one as fragile as a screen door, between them.

She went to the bedroom, opened the bureau drawer and took out the small, squarish box wrapped in brown paper. She swallowed and cradled the box against her chest.

It was hard for her to believe this simple brown-wrapped box contained the mortal remains of a being as sensitive, complicated and singular as Jimmie. She had never done anything like this before, and the task suddenly seemed too much for her, too emotionally charged.

She returned to the screen door and Zane swung it open for her. The dog tried to follow, but Kelly turned, giving it a stern look over her shoulder. "No," she said firmly. "You stay here."

The dog's ears sank in unhappiness, bereavement filled her eyes and her tail almost stopped wagging.

"Let her come," Zane said, unsmiling. It was as much an order as a request.

Kelly looked at him with resentful surprise. "This is a solemn occasion. We don't need a dog that dances and grins."

He shook his head once, briefly but eloquently. "Jimmie loved that dog. He took her in. Let her come."

Drat the man, he was probably right, Kelly thought. She looked again at the dog's face. Somehow, the silly thing's eloquent eyes had achieved an expression of almost pure tragedy.

"Oh, all right," she muttered. "Come on, dog."

All traces of tragedy vanished. Cavorting wildly, the dog shot out the open door and pranced around them in frenzied joy. Kelly saw Zane glance at the box she still cradled against her chest, but he said nothing.

"Where do we go? How do we get there?" she asked.

The sun was sinking lower, and its rays gilded his profile. "It's a place called Blue Heron Cove," he answered tonelessly. "We'll go by canoe."

"Canoe?" Kelly asked apprehensively. She had never in her life been in a canoe.

He said nothing, only led her toward the pebbled shore. His long, silvery canoe was pulled up so that more than half of it was settled on dry land.

Wordlessly he pushed it so all of it was in the water, its length resting parallel to the shore. Kelly watched the complicated working of his muscles beneath the thin cloth of the blue-gray shirt. Once more, against her will, she found herself admiring the economy of his movements.

He raised himself to his full height again and looked down at her silently. Zane's silences and long, probing looks always unnerved Kelly. "Well," she asked testily. "What now?"

He raised one eyebrow in a gesture that told her she had missed the obvious. "Get in," he said, the same note of testiness in his own voice.

The canoe bobbed up and down, up and down on the water.

She frowned slightly. *"How?"* she asked.

"You just get in," he said from between his teeth.

She hesitated. She tried putting one foot into the back end but that made the front end veer more sharply into the water, bobbing more wildly than before. Because she was guarding the box so tightly, she couldn't use her arms for balance. Hastily she withdrew her foot.

"I've never done this," she said, clutching the box more closely. "I don't know how—"

"Oh, good grief, how can anybody who swims as much as you be afraid of getting wet?" he asked, his mouth curling down at one corner. Before she could protest, he picked her up, swinging her into his arms as easily as if she were a child. Disregarding his riding boots and jeans, he waded into the water halfway up to his shins.

Kelly, startled, marveled at his sheer physical strength. She was not a small woman, but he handled her as easily—and as carelessly—as if she were a long-limbed rag doll. She stared, somewhat in awe, at his rugged, solemn face, but he did not so much as glance at her in return.

The heat of his hands burned through her clothes and tingled her flesh. The muscles of his wide chest moved powerfully against her shoulder. It sent an unwanted thrill quaking through her, one she resented. He settled her in the front seat, then gripped the canoe's edge, holding it in place.

"Now," he said. "Call the dog."

Kelly didn't like his peremptory tone, and gave him a look that told him so. He didn't see it. He was staring determinedly off toward the other shore.

Oh, for heaven's sake, she thought, half in anger, half in embarrassment, *let's get this over.*

She whistled for the dog and called. The animal sped toward them at a dead run, then stopped short, almost skidding, when she realized that Kelly, by the strange means of the boat, was in the water. She stood staring at Kelly helplessly, then wagged her tail hesitantly and began to tremble.

"Dog," Zane said impatiently, "get into the boat. In the *boat.*"

"She's afraid of water," Kelly offered.

Zane swore softly, waded to shore, picked up the dog and carried her to the canoe. Unceremoniously he dumped her to its bottom. The dog stood and looked around in bewilderment. "Poor Pollyanna," Kelly said, shaking her head. Pollyanna's brown ears were laid back in apprehension.

Zane clamped his mouth shut more harshly than before, walked the canoe more deeply into the water, then got in with one swift, feral movement. He took up the paddle, and with a few powerful thrusts was propelling them forward.

The water coursed from his tall boots. It trickled into the canoe's bottom and snaked its way toward Pollyanna, who stepped backward daintily from it. The dog eased her way to Kelly and jumped up beside her on the narrow seat, shivering. For once the animal's tail was not wagging, but hung limp between her legs. The farther the canoe sped from shore, the more miserable the dog looked.

"What's wrong with her?" Zane asked, eyeing the dog as he stroked the canoe toward the middle of the lake.

"I told you," Kelly said. She loosed one arm from the box to put it around the trembling Pollyanna. "She doesn't like water. Don't look so stormy. You're the one who wanted to bring her, not me."

He gave both of them a quelling look.

Kelly straightened her back. Powered by Zane's strokes, the canoe went so swiftly that she was a bit uneasy herself. They rode extremely low in the water, and so smoothly that it seemed to her the canoe was some sort of tame water animal that bore them away. The sensation was eerie.

"Is it far?" she asked, hugging the dog closer to her. The animal was still shaking.

Zane shook his head curtly. "Fifteen minutes. Make that dog sit on the bottom. She'll fall out."

Kelly tried to urge Pollyanna to move, but the dog would have none of it. She laid her ears farther back, rolled her eyes until the whites showed, and huddled more firmly against Kelly's side.

Zane looked at the creature and the corners of his mouth turned down farther. "Only Jimmie would have taken up with a dog like that," he muttered.

"Yes," she said, hugging the animal closer. "Only Jimmie." She hugged the box more tightly, too. This was it, she thought, her formal goodbye to Jimmie. It seemed neither real nor possible. She stared at the cliffs, gold and green and shadowed in the twilight.

They were beautiful and peaceful, and something about the way the light played on their ancient faces woke deep and aching emotions in Kelly. How many times had Jimmie made this journey? How many times had he and Zane made it together? Now he would be joining this beauty he had looked on so often, becoming one with it.

She stole a glance at Zane and saw his gaze was fastened on her with its usual disconcerting steadiness. She knew her expression was sad, and struggled to compose it into something more neutral, less revealing. She set her jaw and blinked back the tears she felt rising.

"So," Zane said, his voice as cool and studied as the expression she assumed, "tell me about your writing. I've got your books, by the way. Jim loaned them to me. But I never got around to reading them. Kids' books aren't exactly up my alley. So tell me about them."

There was just enough of a taunt in his remarks to bring the spark back to Kelly's eyes. "I'm sure you'd hate them. They're optimistic. Nobody gets decapitated and no vampires bite anybody. They're meant to make children feel safe and secure. To me, that's what books are for. To make you feel better."

He shrugged and kept up the smooth, steady thrusts of the paddling. He raised a skeptical eyebrow. "You're partly right. Books are supposed to make you *feel*. And kids have more kinds of feelings than most people want to admit."

Kelly turned her attention back to the towering cliffs. "What makes you such an expert on children? Do you have some hidden away somewhere?"

The words had popped out of her mouth before she'd thought of Mavis Pruer's charges and the wisdom of uttering such things. She was embarrassed to have spoken so boldly of what had been whispered and was glad that she wasn't looking at him.

But he answered the question as glibly as she'd asked it. "None that I know of."

A chill gripped her heart, and its coldness spread painfully through her chest. She knew his reply was a standard wisecrack, but she didn't find it funny. She wondered what her own father had said after he had left when someone asked him if he had any children. Had he answered with such a pat and evasive joke?

"Besides," he went on, "what difference does it make if I have kids? I *was* a kid."

Kelly hugged Pollyanna closer to her. The dog hadn't stopped trembling and pressed against her fearfully. Kelly still refused to look at Zane. "I'm sure you *weren't* a typical child. You probably spent all day playing with little plastic guillotines and wearing wax monster fangs."

He laughed disdainfully. "I was so typical I'd make you sick. I grew up in a little town in Missouri. My father was a policeman and my mother was a Sunday-school teacher. I was taught to believe in truth, justice, goodness, happy endings and that virtue would be rewarded. Even then I knew there was more to life than they were telling me. Yeah, I believed there might be such a thing as real evil in the world—call it what you want, monster or a demon. Whatever name you give it, it's there. Kids aren't that easily fooled—not by people and not by books."

His voice had grown so bitter that Kelly watched him almost warily. "Your parents didn't mean to *fool* you, you know," she said after a moment. "They were just trying to protect you. That's what parents do. I hope you don't resent them for that."

His face turned brooding and he made a sound of impatience. "I don't resent them. I feel sorry for them, that's all. They fooled themselves, too."

"What do you mean?" she asked.

"My father thought our world was a sane and kindly place. It was his job to keep it that way. But he couldn't. He was shot when I was eighteen."

"Shot?" A shudder of cold ran through her and she drew the dog closer to her. Was this violence against his father what had plunged Zane into a world of such dark imagining?

"Every cop's nightmare," he said from between his teeth. "One night he stopped an out-of-state car on the edge of town. It had a back light burned out, that was all. He walked over to give them a warning. They shot him, point-blank. Twice. A couple of cheap grifters wanted for fraud and forgery. They left him lying in the road like a dog. He didn't die. But he never walked again."

His brows were drawn together, the set of his mouth stormy. Kelly looked at him in mute questioning, her chest tight with compassion for him and his family.

"They got caught, the couple who shot him," Zane said, his lip curled in contempt. "A man and a woman. He got ten years and was out on parole in five. She got five years and was out in ten months. My mother had been sick before it all happened. It was the same year I—got hurt. Overseas. She worked so hard and worried so much she had a stroke. She died less than a year after he was shot. She was dead, and he was a prisoner in a wheelchair for the next sixteen years of his life. The people who shot him were out free, walking around on two good legs. They still are, for all I know. And are still probably forging and stealing. So much for law, order, sanity and justice. So much for goodness and happy endings. And so much for virtue being rewarded."

He gave another mirthless laugh, his mouth still crooked in disgust.

"I'm sorry," Kelly said. The words sounded stupid and inadequate to her. She wanted to ask him how he had been hurt overseas, but sensed he didn't want to talk about it. She tried for what she hoped was a more neutral topic. "Is that why—why you write the way you do?"

The anger he'd suppressed flashed briefly in his eyes, focusing on her. "No. It's not. Don't psychoanalyze me. I write the way I do because I *like* to. I always liked to. The dark side always called me. It always will. I'd rather look into it and understand it than ignore it, that's all. You remind me of my folks. You'd rather pretend it's not there."

She felt stung, rebuffed. She'd offered him her sympathy, awkward as it was, but he'd refused it and given her harshness and criticism in return. He was a cold man, and she should have known better than to show him kindness.

Raising her chin higher, she gave him the calmest of glances. "So—I want to give people pleasant dreams—but you'd rather give them nightmares. That somehow makes me the villain and you the hero. How interesting."

She turned to face the cliffs again. The sky above them was deep blue, almost lavender, and the voluptuous curves of the clouds were gilded with a hundred subtle shades of molten gold. Why think of terror when there was so much beauty in the world? she wondered in perplexity. "It's—wrong—to think of—unpleasant things," she said, almost to herself. "Why? What for?"

"Kelly."

He said it with such emphasis she found herself turning to meet his gaze again. His eyes looked almost black, and the soft light made his craggy features seem harder.

"I love one kind of fantasy—the same kind Jimmie did. You love another. Each has its place. You want to write books that make people feel better. I don't want to write ones that make them feel *worse,* for God's sake. I just want to make them feel, period."

She sighed and looked down at the trembling dog. "How can terrifying somebody make them feel better?" she asked softly. "What good can it possibly do?"

"Listen," he said earnestly. "Do you know the word *catharsis?* The ancient Greeks used it. It meant a cleansing. That's what a good horror story does. It cleans out all those vague, shapeless fears that haunt the back of the mind. It gives them, at last, a recognizable face. We can see what scares us and we can fight it. Good versus evil. The greatest conflict in the world.''

Kelly shrugged hopelessly. "I wouldn't want my students to know the things you write about. They're too young. They'd be terrified.''

"That's right," Zane almost growled. "I don't write for six-year-olds. I write for adults, people like Jimmie. People who'd face their demon if only their demon had a face.''

She gave him a fragile, bitter smile. "That's your job? You're the man who gives the demons faces?''

He stared at her a long moment, then sighed harshly. "Yes," he said. "I try. For a little while, at least. For the length of a book.''

"A little while," she said, shaking her head. "Temporarily. But you can't do any good in the long run. You can't really chase the demons away. Your books can't change what happened to your parents. They couldn't help Jimmie—not permanently, not really.''

"Kelly," he said from between his teeth, "I can't write to cure the evils of the world. That gift wasn't given to me. All I can do is entertain people in a certain way. I'm not ashamed of what I do. Don't try to make me be.''

She shook her head again, with more emotion than before. "Look, we're arguing again. We said we wouldn't and we shouldn't, not at a time like this. It's not right." She paused, took a deep breath and licked her lips. "And it's not," she said, her throat tightening again, "what Jimmie would have wanted.''

Zane looked at her, sitting there with the cliffs and the golden sky behind her. Her back was straight, but her head was bowed, and he could see real sorrow on her face. The sun's setting rays made her hair seem to have a fine aureole of fire around it, like an angel's.

Why, he wondered, had he told her about his parents, about the shooting? He never spoke of it; he hated talking about it. Why had he tried to tell her, of all people?

And why did he keep trying to justify to her what he did for a living? Thousands of people admired his work. Why should he care if one stubborn woman scorned it?

Wearily he turned away so he wouldn't have to see how the dusky air gilded her shoulders or turned the white of her camisole to the soft color of topaz. He had tried to make her understand, and he couldn't. He was sick of it.

She raised her eyes once more to meet his, which were hard and disapproving. She wished he could understand how deeply she felt about these issues, but she couldn't bear to argue any longer. She came from a bookish family. Zane and Jimmie loved one kind of fantasy. She had been raised to love a different sort. Zane found her views worthless, and that was that.

"You're right," he said, the line of his mouth severe. "He wouldn't want us to fight. Especially not now."

She took another deep breath. "What do you suppose he'd want us to talk about?" Maybe, she thought, they should be exchanging fond reminiscences, not heated opinions.

He looked over his shoulder, at the slight wake the canoe left in the glittering water. "Maybe it'd be better if we didn't try to talk at all," he said.

BLUE HERON COVE WAS a small, deep, sheltered bay, walled with soaring cliffs on one side and by a dark green sweep of forest on the other.

Scarves of mist had formed and floated delicately above the water's surface, giving the place a mystical, almost enchanted look. Kelly was startled by a harsh cry and then saw a great blue heron winging from the trees on the shore to fly across the lake. She almost gasped when a second heron followed the first, its great wings beating silently.

Zane set down the paddle and looked after the birds, hooking his thumbs in his belt. "This is it," he said. "Those herons have lived here for years."

The canoe floated in the cove's middle, barely moving. The dog quivered and looked nervous. Kelly found she was holding the box in both arms again, almost embracing it.

"It's—it's beautiful," she said, watching how the colors of the sunset reflected on the smooth surface, how the trees and cliffs were mirrored in it. "Is that why he picked this place? Because it's so beautiful?"

Zane gave her a cryptic look and a cynical smile. "He picked it because he caught a thirty-two-pound bass here. I was with him. My God, he crowed about it. 'When I die, put me here, where I caught that bass,' he'd always say."

"Oh," Kelly said tonelessly. She watched the light on the water and knew, deep in her heart, that the fish had had nothing to do with Jimmie's choosing this place. Jimmie had had a passion for natural beauty, a passion she was only starting to understand.

"Do you want to say anything?" he asked, watching her. "The traditional 'few words.'"

Suddenly her throat choked again. "I don't think I can," she said honestly, her voice shaking. "I don't think I can do this at all."

"Here," he said gruffly, stretching out his hand. "I'll do it. And I'll say something. It seems like something should be said."

Swallowing hard, she handed him the box. His fingers brushed hers, and that touch, as slight as it was, set her emotions even more on edge. She hugged the dog with both arms, glad now that she was there.

"Jimmie loved books and he loved nature," Zane said, opening the box. His face was solemn and his voice strong but quiet. "So I guess this is appropriate."

He took a deep breath and began to quote Wordsworth.

"Though nothing can bring back the hour
Of splendour in the grass, of glory in the flower,
We will grieve not, rather find

Strength in what remains behind..."

Kelly swallowed hard, recognizing the poem. Zane went on in the same quiet rhythmic voice, faultlessly, never stumbling on a line or missing a word.

Kelly's heart clenched like a fist tensing against pain and some emotion deeper than pain. She had been unable to speak at all.

But Zane had known what to say. The words were not only beautiful, but right. They were the perfect words for Jimmie, the ones he would have wanted.

Slowly Zane poured the ashes into the still water. "Goodbye, my friend," he said softly. "You've left behind the demons and monsters. Rest easy now. Be in peace."

Kelly, pale and trembling, watched him as the last of the fine, gray ashes disappeared.

He turned his eyes to hers again. "Are you all right?"

"Yes," she lied, hanging on to the dog even more tightly.

"No, you're not," he said, disgust in his voice. He dug into his pocket and thrust a white handkerchief in her direction. "Here, damn it, cry. I can't stand watching you be brave. Just cry and be done with it, will you?" He extended his arm even farther in her direction, the motion almost angry. "Take it," he repeated in a harsh tone.

Kelly tried to glare at him and failed. Keeping her back straight, she took the handkerchief. Very carefully she hid her eyes in it so he couldn't see them and she couldn't see him. Then, to her chagrin, she burst into tears and wept like a child. The emotions she had repressed so long overwhelmed her.

Zane turned away and picked up the paddle. She was sitting straight and proper as the schoolmarm she was, sobbing like a little kid, one arm still around that foolish, quaking dog.

He dipped the paddle in the water, putting all his strength into the first strokes to take them away from the cove. Under his breath he swore, then thanked heaven they were in a canoe. Otherwise he would have taken her in his arms. He didn't want to think about that. It made no sense. He didn't want to think about it at all.

CHAPTER SIX

RESOLUTELY KELLY DRIED her eyes. The crying had over-taken her like a summer thundershower, swiftly and intensely. Then, like a storm, its power passed, and she was ashamed to have let Zane see her so emotionally vulnerable.

She scrubbed at her cheeks, then crumpled the handkerchief into a soggy ball, clenching it as hard as she could.

"Doesn't it hurt?" he asked with acid wryness. "Keeping your back that straight all the time?"

She cast him a reproving look, half-grateful that he wasn't being kind. "No," she said shortly. "Of course, it doesn't *hurt.*"

"In a canoe you should be more languid," he said, his eyebrow raised in critical disdain. "And you shouldn't be ashamed of crying. A little show of emotion once in a while doesn't kill you, you know."

Kelly gave a careless shrug. It hadn't been a little show of emotion; it had been an embarrassingly large one, and she knew it. She patted the dog and gazed up at the sky. The clouds had turned to dull purplish gray and the sun was rapidly vanishing behind the cliffs.

"How do you remember it?" she asked, just to say something. "All that poetry?"

It was his turn to shrug. "I just do." His wide shoulders shifted each time he moved the paddle from one side to the other. The canoe sped like a silent arrow through the darkening water.

She said nothing. She studied the sky again and nibbled at her lower lip nervously. The handkerchief was still crushed in her hand.

"What's the matter?" he asked sardonically. "Didn't you think I'd know any poetry? Did you think I spent all my time reading horror comics? Or that I'd only know the kind of poems written on locker-room walls?"

That was precisely what she'd thought, but she was not about to admit it. "It just didn't occur to me that you'd be carrying something like that around in your head," she said.

"Ah," he returned, satire lacing his words, "I carry a great many things around in this head. I know how you imagine my brain—a cheap haunted house with bats hanging from the ceiling and tarantulas lurking in the corners. But I've been known to entertain a noble thought or two. Not for *long,* of course."

"Of course," she agreed. In spite of herself she was impressed by what he had done. It was not just that he could quote Wordsworth; it was that he had known exactly what lines to quote. His sensitivity surprised her and she didn't like contemplating it. Still nonplussed, she changed the subject again.

"A woman showed up today. About sixty, a white-haired little lady. In the rental cabin. A Mavis Pruer. She knew Jimmie. She was quite upset when she found out that he...when she found out. Did he ever say anything about her?"

He raised his eyebrows slightly, shook his head. "Not that I recall offhand. Jim wasn't much interested in little white-haired ladies."

Kelly shifted on the small seat, her arm still around Pollyanna's neck. "She said she stayed here last summer, too."

"I wasn't around last summer. I had some tricky business arrangements to take care of. Different people rent that house all year round. They come and go."

"She talks as if she knew him well," Kelly said, pushing back a stray tendril of hair. A breeze had come up, making the surface of the lake shiver and ripple. "I wondered—well—I just wondered about her and him, that's all."

Zane gave a short laugh. "He must have just been neighborly—since she was older. He was usually shy with what he called 'respectable women.' Jim usually found his women in bars. That was part of the problem."

Kelly blushed. It was a side of Jimmie's character that she hadn't come to terms with. "Well, he seems to have talked to this one quite a bit," she said. Mentally she added, *And he talked to her about you.*

"Oh, Jim was friendly," Zane said half-laughingly. "A man can be friendly and shy at the same time. He just never thought he had much to offer a good woman."

"He could have," Kelly said with feeling. "He could have been a wonderful husband, a wonderful father, if he'd straightened out his life."

"If, Kelly, *if.* It wasn't that easy. The war cut into him deeply, in more ways than one. It did to a lot of us."

His statement startled her. She looked at him more intently, frowning slightly. "Us? You were over there, too? I didn't think you'd be old enough."

"I made it for the end," he said grimly. "It was enough."

"You were wounded, too?" she asked, frankly curious.

"Yes. But nothing like Jim. It was the summer my father was shot—a lousy year—God, what a year."

"The people who shot him," she asked hesitantly, "don't you know what happened to them?"

His face was rigid with bitterness. "People like that, they change their names a dozen times—they drift here—there—who knows? Who cares? I don't want to talk about it. Forget it."

He went silent, concentrating on paddling.

Kelly watched his face, shadowy now in the failing light. He was a man conversant with horror, who lived with it on a daily basis, and it had struck his personal life more than once. It must have uprooted and destroyed the sane, orderly life he'd been taught to believe in. Such things would play havoc with a man's mind. What would it do to his soul? she wondered.

"Jimmie didn't like to talk about it, either," she said softly.

"I know."

Kelly sighed. Somewhere a fish leaped and splashed. The dog stood shakily on the seat, looking nervously into the distance. It seemed to see something.

"Make her sit," Zane warned out of the side of his mouth. "She can't keep her balance there—she hasn't got enough footing."

"I can't," Kelly said, pushing down ineffectually on the dog's rear end. "Jimmie never exactly trained her, you know. I think she sees something—"

The dog strained as it stared at something in the water. Kelly scanned the lake until she, too, spotted a dark object bobbing in the ripples. She frowned. "What is it?"

Zane paddled closer to the spot where the last rays of the sun reflected from whatever it was that broke the lake's surface. The dog began to shake with excitement.

"Oh, *great,*" Zane said. "It's an empty Pepsi bottle. What a dog. It gets excited over Pepsi bottles."

Kelly looked, her heart sinking slightly. The dog was trying to dance in place, its eyes fastened fanatically on the half-submerged two-liter plastic bottle. "Settle down," Kelly ordered, trying to stroke Pollyanna into calmness. "It's just a big plastic bottle. It—"

Afterward Kelly was never sure what had happened. Did Pollyanna jump? Did she fall?

Suddenly there was a splash and the dog sank into the hated water, then rose, frantic and wild eyed. Kelly reached for her and Zane reached for Kelly, and an instant later they were all in the water. The canoe had rolled over and the world had turned from solid to liquid.

Kelly sputtered, wiped the water out of her eyes and grabbed at the dog, which was swimming in crazed circles.

Zane surfaced beside her, swearing and struggling to right the canoe. The paddle floated lackadaisically on the ripples, and so did the two green cushions that were supposed to be used for flotation devices.

Zane swore again, with a great deal of imagination and passion. "Are you all right, damn it?"

"I'm fine," Kelly said, holding the dog securely so she wouldn't struggle. "Are you?"

"I'm as fine as anybody who's just been swamped by a bloody bottle hound from hell. Have you got her?"

"Yes," Kelly answered.

"Then drown her," he ordered. "Most useless dog on God's green earth." He swore again as he managed to heave the canoe back into its correct position.

Zane then swam to gather the cushions and oar and threw them back into the canoe. He swam surely and powerfully, as at home in the water as she was.

"A fifty-dollar flashlight just went to the bottom," he muttered. "And a pair of expensive binoculars. *And* my favorite sunglasses."

He swore once more as he struggled out of his boots and threw them into the canoe with more force than was necessary. They lay there, half-covered by the water in the bottom.

"Can you handle that dismal excuse for a dog?" he asked, blinking the water from his eyes.

"She's fine as long as I keep her supported. She's terrified, though." The dog shook harder than ever in her arms, but she looked up at Kelly with desperate trust in her eyes.

"Good," he said, his voice full of sheer dislike. "Can you get her to shore?"

"Easy," Kelly said. "Where?"

He nodded toward a rocky stretch of shore between two cliffs. "There. By the dead tree. I'll get the canoe there, then we can empty it and regroup. Fool dog."

Kelly had taken a lifesaving course, but she'd never tried to save a dog. She turned on her back, kept one arm hooked firmly around Pollyanna and began to backstroke toward the shore. Zane, clinging to the side of the boat with one arm, started taking vigorous strokes with the other. His teeth were gritted and his face stony.

"It was your idea to bring Pollyanna out here. Not mine," she reminded him, swimming far more easily than he could. The dog lay against her chest like a baby, all four feet in the air. "I wanted to leave her home. Remember?"

"How would you like to be marooned?" he asked acidly.

"I'm merely pointing out a fact," Kelly said with evil sweetness. "You should appreciate this little incident. Terror and emotion are your specialties, aren't they? Well, Pollyanna's terrified of the water and she got emotional over a bottle. Now you're a tad emotional yourself, if I do say so."

"I'm beginning to understand why you've never married," he muttered.

"Why?" Kelly asked innocently. Now that she was over the shock of tipping, the water was warm and actually pleasant. It felt good to exert herself physically and she was almost enjoying the challenge of keeping the dog quiet and secure.

"Your little tongue is sharp and venomous. Like an adder's fang."

Kelly answered by sassily sticking out her tongue at him. "Take that," she said. The water had shocked all other emotions from her system and made her feel almost frisky. "And that."

He was not amused.

She gained the shallow water before he did and let Polly-anna swim the last few yards herself. Kelly stood, strug-gling to get her footing on the rocky bottom and waded, her wet clothes clinging to her body, onto shore. The dog gal-loped insanely back and forth along the bank, as if trying to outrun its wetness.

Kelly turned and, pushing her drenched hair back, watched Zane reach the shallow water. He stood, then half tugged, half carried the canoe, sloshing toward the shore, his shoulders swaying with the effort. With a grunt he dragged the canoe up onto a slab of rock, unloaded it, then tipped it, spilling out the water.

He swore again. "A Pepsi bottle. A rabbit could walk up and spit in that dog's eye and she'd just sit there. A squirrel could jump up and down on her head and she'd let it. So what's it in her nature to hunt? Pepsi bottles, in the name of all that's holy."

Kelly gathered her hair in her hands and tried to wring it out. She was soaked through, and the breeze made her chilly. "Maybe she doesn't like litter," she said lightly. "Maybe it's her instinct to attack it."

He sat down, emptied the water out of his boots and pulled them on. "Don't try to justify this. She's a Pepsi at-tack dog and that's it. Maybe you could sell her to the Coca-Cola company."

Kelly gave him a smile, a fleeting one, but a smile never-theless. It was the first time he'd ever seen her smile, even a little, and it gave something in his chest an unexpected wrench. She had a wide smile, very white, and she had dim-ples, something he hadn't expected.

She looked down at her empty hands, her smile gone. "I dropped your handkerchief. I'm sorry. I'll buy you another one."

He gave a long sigh. "Forget it," he said. "It's no big deal."

"And I'm sorry about your flashlight and binoculars," she said, looking away, toward the ridged wall of the cliff. "I suppose I should replace those, too. After all, she's my dog now. So it's my responsibility."

He rose from his sitting position and tucked his shirt back into his jeans. It had come out while he was swimming. He looked at her profile in the twilight, but couldn't tell if she wanted to laugh or cry again.

No wonder she had joked when they'd capsized, he thought. That's what she'd most needed: comic relief after all the strain and emotion of saying her last goodbyes to Jimmie. Yes, he wished she'd smile again. He wished it almost fiercely.

She put her hands on her upper arms, hugging herself slightly, as if she were cold. The wet, white camisole was molded to her upper body, and her jeans clearly outlined the sweep of her long legs. She had lost the white hair ribbon, and her long chestnut hair hung in wet, unruly waves.

Pollyanna had found a patch of grass and was rolling in it, drying herself with all the vigor of one demented. Zane took a step toward Kelly.

"You don't pay for anything," he said, his voice so low he almost growled the words. "You were right. It was my fault. I shouldn't have made you bring her."

Kelly looked up at him warily. His straight brown hair looked almost black when it was wet and it hung in his eyes. The soaked shirt hugged his big shoulders and pasted itself to the hard muscles of his chest and stomach. He gave her a crooked half smile.

"I wasn't too dignified, was I?" he asked, raising one eyebrow in rue.

She shook her head, gazing at the shadowy planes of his face. "No. You weren't."

"Neither were you," he drawled, putting his hands on his hips. "You should have seen yourself. You grabbed for the dog and ended up grabbing water. You came up spitting and sputtering like a fountain."

She smiled slightly, a close-lipped smile of self-mockery. "Well, I never heard anything make a bigger splash than you did. It sounded like a moose hitting the water. And then you swore. You were *awful.*"

"I was magnificent. And then that dog, swimming around in circles like some windup toy gone crazy."

She shook her head, still smiling the close-lipped smile. They both turned and looked at Pollyanna, who was busy giving herself a bath, licking away all traces of lake water from her flanks. Then they turned their eyes back to each other.

"I guess it's not the proper way to end a solemn occasion, is it?" she asked, her smile fading again.

He shrugged, pushed his hair back out of his eyes. He had a fine forehead, she thought, just high and wide enough to give him an air of formidable intelligence.

"Maybe," he said, stirring a heap of pebbles with his boot, "it's the perfect way to end a solemn occasion. At least this one."

"What do you mean?"

He cocked one hip and stared at the darkening sky. "I mean," he said, "Jimmie would have laughed his head off if he could have seen us—the three of us all ending up in the drink. He'd have laughed till it hurt."

She looked up at him shyly and smiled, more fully this time. "He would, wouldn't he? He'd say, 'This is how you end my funeral?'"

"Well, you did look funny," he said, grinning himself. "That dog did some sort of swan dive, and you were right behind her, like a ballerina for a minute—before you fell on your face in the water."

Kelly laughed. "I didn't even know what had happened. One second I was in the canoe and the next one I was un-

derwater. And then you were there, too, doing your flounder imitation.''

"Flounder?'' he teased.

"Yes, flounder,'' she insisted. ''Glub-glub-blub. Splash-
splash-splash. Grump-grump-grump. A very grouchy
flounder.''

He laughed. ''Did you see the look in that dog's eyes? It
was like she'd just seen Godzilla.''

She laughed again, too. ''You should have seen the look
in *your* eyes. You were like Zeus about to hurl the lightning
bolt. I mean, we're talking *titanic* anger here.''

"Jim probably engineered this from the Other Side. I
wouldn't put it past him. He's probably rolling around the
floor of Heaven right now, saying, 'Look at those two
drowned rats.'''

Kelly giggled helplessly, looking down at her sodden
clothes. ''We do look pretty bad.''

She looked at him and was surprised to see an expression
of slightly horrified disbelief cross his face. ''What's
wrong?'' she asked.

He frowned, reached into his shirt pocket and pulled out
a tiny minnow, live and less than two inches long. It wrig-
gled in the palm of his hand.

Kelly exploded into laughter. He did, too, and kept
laughing as he walked to the shore and released the thrash-
ing little fish.

Kelly laughed so hard she had to sit down on the shore.
The emotions she'd felt before had been extremely intense;
now it was as if they'd found some release at last. Her
laughter threatened to shake her whole body.

Zane lowered himself to sit beside her, laughing, too.

She looked him in the eye and dissolved into even greater
hysterics. She put one hand on her stomach, clutching it.
"You—you—you had a fish—in your pocket,'' she managed to sputter, then had to cross her arms over her knees

and bury her face against them, hoping she could stop laughing.

He, too, was chuckling so hard he seemed almost out of control. "I wouldn't have had a fish in my pocket," he objected, "if your dog hadn't chased the ferocious Pepsi bottle."

"Oh, don't say that," Kelly begged, her face still buried. She banged her fist against her knee, hoping it would stop her from laughing, but it didn't. She was giddy, helpless, possessed.

"Say what?" he demanded.

"Say *that*. Pep-Pep-Pep—"

"Pepsi," he said wickedly. "Pepsi. She saw this vicious killer Pepsi bottle and she sprang to save us from it—no wonder Jimmie named her Fang."

"Stop! Stop!" Kelly pleaded. She had laughed so hard she had a stitch in her side. She felt weak with jubilant silliness, used up and convulsed by it. She sank on her back and kept laughing, clutching her aching ribs. "Don't make me laugh anymore," she giggled. "My side hurts. My *face* hurts." She put one hand to her jaw, for she had laughed so hard the muscles in her cheeks were starting to smart.

All she could see was a graying sky full of plum-colored clouds, and then she could not see that. A dark shape blocked them, Zane's. He had leaned over her; his face was only inches from hers.

"Are you going to be all right? Or will I end up saying a few last words over you, too?"

He had been smiling, but as he stared down at her, the merriment left his eyes and something else replaced it. Kelly's laughter died. She stared up at him, still smiling, as if in reflex.

"You're beautiful when you smile," he said softly. "But when you laugh, you're gorgeous."

Her hair was fanned out on the stone, and he lifted a strand of it, using its tip to trace the line of her jaw. Her smile faded, and she could only look into his eyes, her lips slightly parted. She was still breathing hard because of her laughing fit, but now her heart jumped wildly in her chest.

He put his hand to her face and gently brushed the hair back from her forehead, then rested his fingers against her chin.

He said nothing, yet she felt somehow that they were speaking without words.

I'm going to kiss you, his eyes said.

I know.

I didn't want this to happen.

Neither did I.

But you'll let me, won't you?

Yes. Yes.

You want me to, don't you?

Yes. I do. Oh, yes.

Her eyes flickered shut as his lips descended and found hers. His mouth was at first cool, then warm, then hot upon her own, and so gentle that all her senses quivered at the unexpected tenderness. For a moment his lips were very still against hers, as if the two of them needed a moment to explore the strange and fragile connection between them.

Slowly his mouth grew more mobile, more expressive, more demanding. His hand slid beneath her head, cushioning it; his fingers laced in the cool dampness of her hair. His other hand closed over her bare, cool shoulder.

Through her wet camisole she could feel the heat and hardness of his chest, and when he drew her nearer to him, the strength of his long thighs stretched against hers. The heat of his body pulsed through his wet clothes and through hers, filling her with warmth.

He lifted her face, pressing it more intimately against his, and when she gasped in confusion and pleasure against his lips, she tasted the heat and moisture of his exploring tongue. Shyly she slipped her tongue against his, and when she did, he inhaled sharply, pulling her against him so tightly that for a moment she thought their two bodies might somehow merge into one electric entity.

His mouth trailed from her lips to her throat, exploring and heating its smoothness and hollows, from her throat to her collarbone, tracing and tasting its curve. His hand moved to her side, stroking the slender line of her rib cage before coming to rest just below her breast, as if framing it.

He raised his head and kissed her lips again as his hand moved across her breast to undo the top button of her camisole. Kelly knew she should resist, but she did not. She felt him undo the first button, then slide his fingers against her flesh as he began to unfasten the second.

Vaguely she heard the chatter of claws against stone, and then she felt something cold and wet thrust itself against her cheek. Her eyes flew open in alarm.

Pollyanna had thrown herself on top of them in a frenzy of adoration. If affection was going to be shown, the dog had obviously decided that she would lead the way. She kissed Kelly repeatedly, then jigged about and tried to lavish more kisses on Zane.

He sat up swiftly, pulled Kelly into a sitting position beside him and tried so shove the dog away. Instead the animal flung herself onto Zane's lap and lay there, staring up at him with worshipful eyes, wagging her tail madly.

"This dog," he said between clenched teeth, "has got to go."

"This dog may be smarter than both of us," Kelly breathed, trying to draw away from him. Zane wouldn't let her pull away; he held her fast. "Or maybe Jimmie made that happen, too," she said shakily.

Zane's face went hard and assumed the unreadable expression it sometimes did. "Oh, yes, Jim. Well, I don't suppose he'd mind me comforting you, within reason, but—" He left the sentence unfinished.

This time when Kelly drew back from him, he let her. She scrambled to her feet. Shoving the dog away, Zane also

stood, looking down at Kelly. Pollyanna, although so
roughly abandoned, pranced around them, wanting more
attention.

"I'm ashamed of myself," Kelly said, her voice quaking.
She turned away and stared off into the deepening shadows
that were swallowing the cliffs.

"Look," he said, stepping close behind her. He picked up
a thick wet strand of her hair, making her neck tickle and
prickle.

"Don't." Her voice was sharp.

"Look," he repeated, but he didn't try to touch her again.
"This was a very natural thing to happen. Emotions were
up—"

"Please," Kelly said, suddenly feeling very weary. "Just
take us home. I want to go home."

"All I'm saying is—"

"Home," she said stubbornly, cutting him off. "Take me
home. Now."

He was silent for a long moment. "Fine," he said at last.
"Fine. I'll take you home."

They didn't speak again until he pulled the canoe up to
the shore by Jimmie's house. Kelly was too ashamed. How
could she go through a ceremony honoring Jim and then
twenty minutes later lie willingly in a man's arms?

And yet, she thought, her cheeks fiery with guilt, she had
wanted to lie there, hadn't she? She had fallen down on her
back in her wet and clinging clothes as if in invitation.

No, no, she told herself, she had collapsed in laughter, not
to tease or tempt him. Was that true? She didn't know. She
truly didn't. Trying to know made her head hurt.

He got out of the canoe and gave her a hand to help her
onshore. She didn't want to touch him again, to bring her
flesh into that jolting contact with his. But she knew she'd
have difficulty negotiating her way out of the canoe and so
she had no choice. She took his hand and felt its live warmth
and strength vibrating against her cold fingers. She held the

dog in her other arm and tried to concentrate on that squirming bundle, not on Zane's touch.

He released her hand, then stood looking down at her.

"I've got your books to bring back to you. After that, I won't try to see you again. Unless you want it."

"That's probably best," she said, not looking at him.

"It probably is. Well." He ran his hand over his hair restlessly. "At least we got old Jim where he wanted to be."

"Yes," she said, glancing up. "We did."

He said nothing, merely nodded. He reached out and gave Pollyanna a pat of reluctant affection. Then he turned away from Kelly and she turned away from him.

She heard the soft splash of his canoe as it took to the water again. She put down the dog and walked slowly to the house. Her back was no longer as straight as she had willed it to be all evening long.

Above her the sky was dark now and stars winked through patches in the clouds. A full moon, plump and yellow, was climbing in the sky.

Was a full moon for vampires or for werewolves, she wondered moodily, letting herself into the house. Zane would know. That was his specialty, after all. Monsters and demons, darkness and danger. How could she allow herself to feel attracted to a man so different from her in every way?

"Kelly! Oh, Kelly!" Mavis Pruer's voice chortled merrily from the screened deck of her house. "I came over earlier, but you were gone. But the Jeep was there. Did you just slip away?"

"Yes," Kelly said. "I took a boat ride. With a—a neighbor." She tried to sound polite, but she didn't want to talk. She ached to be alone to sort out her tumbled thoughts and feelings.

"Well, I made some brownies," Mavis said. "I wanted to bring you some. You're too thin, young lady, way too thin. I'll be right over."

Oh, no, Kelly thought miserably, not wanting company. She started to make an excuse, but when she called, "Mavis?" there was no answer. The woman must have already bustled back inside her house.

Quickly Kelly slipped into Jimmie's house, turned on the lights and changed from her wet clothing. She would have liked to take a bath, but there was no time with Mavis arriving. She wrapped a towel around her head, turban-style, and washed her face.

She heard Mavis's tap at the door and went to open it. The woman stumped in, her cane in one hand, a chipped blue-and-white plate of brownies in the other. "Jim used to love my brownies," Mavis said, her eyes twinkling in fond memory. "I said to myself, 'Mavis, he'd want you to put some fat on that niece of his.' I thought we'd have a nice cup of coffee and a little girl talk."

Kelly's smile was strained and she had to keep shooing Pollyanna away from Mavis. She was afraid the dog would leap against the woman's injured leg and hurt her, or knock away her cane and make her fall. Finally she had to scoop the dog up and deposit her outside.

"What a sweet little doggie," Mavis said, settling herself unasked at the kitchen table. Her quick eyes ran over the interior of the house, seeming to catalog all she saw. "Jimmie didn't have her last year. It must be a great comfort, having a watchdog."

Kelly sighed. The woman was determined to visit. Kelly would give her coffee, then beg off, pleading exhaustion. It would be no lie.

"She's no watchdog," Kelly said, putting the kettle on to boil. "She's not good for much, I'm afraid. I'll have to find a home for her. *And* all those cats."

"Cats?" Mavis said brightly. She fluffed her curly white hair. "Why, I wouldn't mind having one of Jimmie's cats. I love cats. It would be such a marvelous reminder of him."

Kelly, who had been spooning instant coffee into a set of mismatched cups, stopped and stared at Mavis in reassessment. Suddenly the woman struck her as kind and wonderfully helpful. "You'd take one of the cats?" Kelly said, hoping she'd heard correctly.

"Maybe even two," Mavis said. "I like those yellow ones. Yes. I have a little house in Fort Smith with a big yard. I've been thinking of getting a cat ever since Mr. Pruer passed away. It gets lonely, you know. Two cats—wouldn't that be marvelous?"

The kettle began to shrill, and Kelly poured hot water into the mugs and sat them on the table. She put out spoons, cream and sugar, and set out plates for the brownies.

"No sugar, no cream," Mavis said, waving them away. "And no brownies. I've munched all evening long." She stretched out the leg with the cast ruefully, an awkward gesture. "Well, when you can't get around or do anything—you eat. I always have loved to cook. And now that I'm alone—well, it's a pleasure to cook for someone else for a change." She sighed, then smiled winningly at Kelly. "Eat up, dear."

Kelly bit into a brownie. She was surprised to find it as hard and tasteless as a brick, but she knew she must somehow choke it down or hurt Mavis's feelings.

"Did you and your friend go swimming, honey?" Mavis asked. She leaned her elbow on the table, her chin on her hand and studied Kelly with disconcerting frankness. She stared at the towel hiding Kelly's hair.

"Yes," Kelly said, "we swam." It wasn't exactly a lie, she thought. But she had no intention of telling the whole truth to this woman, even if she was a potential owner for two of Jimmie's cats.

"Who *is* your friend?" Mavis asked. "Anyone I might know?"

He's the man you warned me about, Kelly wanted to say. "I don't think so," she said instead. She managed to wash down the last of the brownie with a long drink of coffee.

"Have another. You're so thin, you need it," Mavis said, pushing the plate in her direction.

Kelly took another against her will. She broke off a brittle corner and nibbled without enthusiasm.

"I couldn't help but see it was a man," Mavis chirped. "I was sitting out on my deck, watching the stars come out. There are some nice young men around here," she went on. "There's a chicken farmer right across the lake and a lovely young man with a peach orchard down the road. Then Dr. Hardesty spends part of the summer here. Now *there's* a catch for a pretty young girl. Rich, he is. Lonely, poor man. And so nice. Not like that Graye man."

The dull ache that had haunted Kelly's head suddenly turned into a sharp little spear of pain. She had been toying with the brownie, but set it down. She put her hand to her forehead and squinted across the table at Mavis.

"You have a lot to say about the Graye man for not knowing him," she said flatly. She did not mean it as an argument, only a statement of fact.

Mavis took it in her stride, fluffing her hair again. "Only because of Jimmie. He said, 'Mavis, I love that Graye man like a brother, but I wouldn't want him messing with someone like my niece.' That's the truth, honey. He said those very words to me. And that's why I say them to you. Believe me, I thought about it—I'm not usually one to gossip. He sounds like a cousin I had. Such a good friend to a man—but with women? The very devil."

"I see," Kelly said, but she wasn't sure she saw anything clearly. Her headache stabbed her sharply, making her wince.

"Honey," Mavis said after a moment of silence, "you don't look like you feel well. I can tell you've been working hard. This place looks clean as a new bandbox—not the way

I saw it last, with all Jimmie's old books and newspapers all over. You've probably been working *too* hard. Why don't you get to bed. I'll skedaddle on home."

"I'm sorry," Kelly said, rubbing her forehead again. "But maybe you're right. It's been hectic."

She started to rise, but Mavis had already clambered to her feet. Staunchly she stood over Kelly and put her hand on her shoulder, forcing her to stay in the chair. She was a surprisingly strong woman.

"You sit down. I'll be on my way. I'll come back for the plate another time. I know my way out, all righty."

Mavis hobbled to the door with more swiftness than Kelly had imagined possible. Perhaps she went too fast, for she stumbled as she reached the door, but caught herself against the frame and giggled self-consciously.

"Are you all right?" Kelly asked in concern, starting to rise.

"You sit, sit, sit," ordered Mavis with a *tsk-tsk*. "Sometimes I just forget I can't go at the pace I want. Should I let this sweet dog in?"

"Please," Kelly said, although in her present state of confusion and headache, she wasn't sure she would term Pollyanna a "sweet dog."

"I'll lock the door behind me," Mavis said cheerily. "You go to bed now. You look right peaked, as they say down here."

Mavis disappeared, pulling the door tightly shut behind her. Pollyanna came tap-dancing across the linoleum, anxious to get to Kelly as fast as possible. She was wearing her unsettling grin.

"Please," Kelly begged, putting her elbow on the table and her head in her hand. "Not so much adoration. You make me feel like I ought to be an archangel, at least."

She rose and went into the bathroom, shutting out Pollyanna, who, wagging up a storm, wanted to follow her everywhere. She took two aspirin, then took a quick, hot bath to wash the lake water from her hair and body.

Kelly felt better after she dried her hair, although her head felt oddly muzzy. It was as if part of her brain wanted to sleep and part of it was incapable of slumber.

She started a letter to Cissie, explaining again about the safety deposit box and that she was enclosing the signature form card to be signed, along with the key. But she had difficulty concentrating and left the unfinished letter in the typewriter, the card and extra key beside it.

Finally, deciding it was time she turned in, she went into the bedroom, climbed into bed and pulled the sheet around her securely. She fluffed up the pillow, leaned it against the head of the bed and sat back.

Taking a deep breath, she opened the thick black book she had brought to bed with her. Kelly didn't understand what possessed her to want to try to read *Her Demon Lover* now. Zane was the last person she should let herself think about.

And yet, she thought, the muzziness in her head not allowing her to think clearly, and yet... tonight, with the fading light on the lake, she had cried harder than she had ever cried before, laughed harder than she'd ever laughed, and then...

And then she'd kissed and been kissed with more passion than she'd known could exist between a man and a woman. Too much sorrow, too much laughter, too much desire, too much emotion altogether.

So she would read. All her life she'd escaped into a world of books. If it was ironic that she now turned to Zane's book to escape thoughts of Zane, so be it, she thought grimly. Her forehead furrowed in determination, she began to read.

Reading would help her put him into perspective. He was, after all, nothing but a hack writer, a man who exploited melodrama and cheap fear, she told herself. She glanced at her watch. It was ten o'clock. By ten-thirty, as dazed and fatigued as she was, his book would certainly put her to sleep.

But at three o'clock in the morning, Kelly still sat in bed, straight up, unable to stop reading, even though the words blurred before her eyes. She was locked into a story in which a woman's eerie dreams of an immortal lover seemed to be coming true in waking reality, but in a strangely twisted version.

Kelly's eyes burned and her mind swirled with the powerful and complicated currents of the story. She forced herself to quit reading for a while. She got out of bed, padded to the kitchen and ate another of Mavis's rock-hard brownies, then drank a glass of milk.

She returned to bed, snuggling down between the sheets, and took up Zane's book again. He might write about demons, Kelly thought with reluctant admiration, but he wrote about them like an angel. She would stay up all night finishing his book; it was as if it had cast a spell over her, a charm whose power she could not resist.

But despite how compelled she felt, even driven to finish the book, the strange muzziness clouded her brain again. She found her eyes sinking shut, the book falling, still open, on her breast. She just barely managed to roll over and switch off the light. Shutting the book, Kelly curled up with it clasped to her chest like a talisman.

Sleep brought with it strange, vivid dreams that were unconnected to one another, except that in each she found a tall, powerful man with deep gray eyes waiting for her in the mists. But she could not tell if he waited there for good or evil.

CHAPTER SEVEN

KELLY AWOKE LATE, her head achy and her limbs heavy. When she tried to bury her face in the pillow, she felt something sharp press between her breasts. *Book,* she thought hazily. *I fell asleep with a book.*

Reluctantly she rolled over, opening her eyes. Sunlight streamed through the slats of the blinds. Something heavy kept her from moving her feet.

She raised herself painfully on one elbow and saw that Pollyanna had once again slipped onto the foot of the bed. The dog looked at her guiltily, but love everlasting shone out from her eyes and she wagged her tail in adoration.

"Pollyanna," Kelly said, sighing in exasperation, "I'm not worthy of all this devotion. *Please.*"

She thrust her hand beneath the sheet and drew out the book that had wedged its corner into her breastbone. A thick book with a glossy black cover. Zane's book. She stared at it a moment, and her hand almost trembled.

She remembered now how the story had gripped her. It had been hypnotic, poetic, sensual, almost unbearable in its suspense. How could she have fallen asleep? And how would she keep her hands off it today, when she still had a hundred tasks to do? With the story unfinished, she felt somehow incomplete, exiled from its spellbinding world.

That was no way to think, she warned herself. If she admired the story, she would come perilously close to admiring the man. She thrust the book away, laying it on the nightstand, but her fingers still tingled from its touch.

Sitting up, she shook her head to clear it. She didn't want to hold Zane in awe. He was, according to Mavis Pruer's gossip and Kelly's own experience, a demon lover himself.

Memories of the evening before washed over her in a dizzying rush. It was as if for a few hours she had lived with a new, almost supernatural intensity, and her life had burned like a perfect, jewellike flame.

Stop, she told herself fiercely, throwing back the sheet and rising from bed. *Don't think that way.* She swayed a moment, her head throbbing. The fuzziness in her head and heaviness in her limbs almost made her sink back onto the bed. But the moment passed, and she felt almost herself again.

With both hands she smoothed her hair back from her face as she stepped into the main area of the house. She found herself unaccountably drawn to the window. The cliffs blazed palely in the morning sun, the sky was such a bright azure it almost hurt her eyes and a great blue heron waded in the glassy water.

The sight of the heron inflicted a pang. She remembered the herons in that enchanted little cove, remembered Zane's words at twilight for Jimmie, and all the deep emotions those words had awakened.

Zane wrote the way he quoted poetry, Kelly thought, gazing out at the tree-crowned cliffs. He seemed to write effortlessly, flawlessly, never fumbling or going astray. No wonder Jimmie had loved the Farley Collins books.

She had let the covers of the early paperback editions, gory and tasteless, put her off. She had made snap judgments. Because Zane was popular, she had supposed he must be cheap. Because he wrote swiftly, she had supposed he wrote badly. Because he wrote suspense and horror novels, she had believed he wrote the sort of thing beneath her notice.

Without giving him a chance, she had foolishly misjudged him as a writer, and she felt sick when she remembered how, on that terrible day they had met, she had kicked one of his books. All her life she had had high standards and firm opinions, but she had always tried to be fair. She had been anything but fair to Zane.

Her troubled eyes swept the mirrorlike surface of the lake, where cliffs, trees and sky reflected darkly. Had she almost misjudged him as a man? Had he kissed her last night only because she had acted all too obviously like a woman wanting to be kissed? Or had he done it because he saw someone ripe to be exploited? Disturbed, she turned from the window. It was a question she couldn't answer.

He was brilliant, but he had a dark side. Beneath the surface of his easy casualness lurked more intensity than she had ever before encountered. He seemed at once a man happy in the simplicity of the outdoors and a man of great sophistication. His intellect intrigued her as much as his sensuality frightened her.

He was so full of paradoxes that she might never learn the truth about him. But, she asked herself, what did it matter? She might see him once again, no more. What did it matter at all what he really was?

Still, his image haunted her as she drove into the nearest small town. She had finished her letter to Cissie—assuring her again there was no way for anyone except the two of them to get into the safety deposit box—and wanted to mail it, along with the signature form and the key. Her own safety deposit key was tucked securely in her wallet.

She wanted to do everything before she forgot. All the pressures on her were making her absent-minded, inefficient. She'd somehow misplaced Jim's extra house key, which had hung on a nail beside the door. Too many thoughts of Zane, she thought wearily, and not enough about the business at hand.

After she mailed Cissie's letter, she had to find a junk man to haul away the broken and worthless objects cluttering Jimmie's yard. She had more cleaning supplies to buy and needed to talk to a real estate agent about putting the house up for sale.

By the time Kelly reached town, the morning sun beat down brighter and hotter. As she walked the surprisingly crowded sidewalks looking for a real estate agent's office, she found herself already wishing she was back at the lake with its soothing breezes.

Her full-skirted cotton dress had turned limp with the heat. Pushing back her hair, she longed for simplicity and quiet, not this busy street with its sizzling concrete and heat-soaked bricks. She wondered, suddenly, how she had survived life in a city like Cleveland for so long.

But when she remembered the cool, shade-dappled lake, memories of Zane rushed back with such force they were like an assault that left her breathless and more than a little giddy.

She recalled too clearly what she had been struggling to forget. It flooded back, how it felt to be swept into the sheltering strength of Zane's arms, how his fingers had laced through her wet hair, drawing her face nearer his. She recalled the imprint of his long, taut body against hers, and how, even through their soaking clothes, the heat of his flesh had warmed her.

She bit her lower lip in something akin to pain, remembering how he had lowered his face to hers and touched her lips so gently for such a long moment. Then the kiss had turned into something wilder and even sweeter. All the ways he had touched her came back in a memory of aching exactitude.

Would he really come back again, as he had said? Would he bring her books? What would he say if he did? What would she say to him?

She paused in front of a bookstore. As if to mock her, a display of the latest Farley Collins novel decorated the window. The cover was scarlet this time, the script of the title gold. *Illusions,* read the gilded flowing letters. By Farley Collins.

Prodded by impulse, Kelly took a deep breath and plunged into the dark coolness of the shop. An aging white poodle lay sleeping next to the counter and an angular man in shirtsleeves stood next to the cash register. Everything about him seemed sharp and pointed, his nose, his cheekbones, his chin, his long, pale fingers.

"May I help you?" he asked, looking over the tops of his glasses. His voice was as sharp as the rest of him.

"I—I wondered," Kelly said, her heart beating shallowly, "about that book in the window, *Illusions.* I've heard that the author, Farley Collins, lives around here. In this state, at least. Is it true?"

The man gave her a long, bored look. "I haven't the foggiest," he said. "I'm hardly what you'd call a fan."

"Oh," Kelly murmured, embarrassed. "I just wondered. I'd heard—a rumor. You know."

"Nobody knows where Farley Collins lives, as far as *I* know," the man said archly. "And I, for one, couldn't care less. Horror is not my *métier.* Literature is. Farley Collins's books, however, help pay my rent. He's a crass commercialist, and I put up with him for my own crassly commercial reasons." Delicately he raised his nose to signify contempt.

Kelly's eyebrow shot up. "Have you ever read him?"

"No. I saw a movie based on one of his early books. It was...words fail me. Unspeakable will have to do, I suppose. I've heard he won't sell to the movies anymore. Perhaps he does have a crumb of taste somewhere."

Kelly stared at him, wondering dully if she had sounded as snobbish to Zane as this man did to her.

"Now if you're interested in *local* writers," the man said, strolling to a nearby section of shelves, "we have them. Dear me, we have them the way a dog has fleas. The university's right down the road, you know. Turn over a rock—or a bar stool—and you'll find a writer. Some are even good."

He was obviously a man who took his pleasure by feeling superior. Kelly stared at the display of books he had shown her in his scoffing way. It was indeed impressive.

"What's your pleasure?" the man asked in the same supercilious tone. "History? Biography? Folklore? Poetry? A mystery, perhaps?"

Kelly bit her lip. "I—is there a man who lives out by the lake who writes? I met him. I—got the impression that he wrote."

The man's mouth pursed sourly. "Oh," he said with maximum sarcasm. "*Him.* That Graye person. At *least* he has the brains to write under another name. What name, he has the decency not to say. He writes Westerns—cheap horse operas, I'm told. Buy those at the drugstore. I certainly don't carry *that* sort of dreck. One has to draw the line *somewhere.*"

Kelly looked at him coolly. She swore she would never again take satisfaction in looking down on others as this man did.

"So what will it be?" the man asked, crisply businesslike again. "Here's a lovely book with color photographs of mushrooms of the region. On sale this week, only $49.95."

"I want the Collins book," she said shortly. "That's all."

The man rolled his eyes, not bothering to hide his distaste. Fuming, Kelly turned away and stared at another section of shelves. No wonder Zane had been so angry with her, she thought. She *had* acted exactly like this haughty, hateful prig of a man. A painful weight swelled in her chest.

She stared almost unseeing at the shelves of children's books. She didn't even know why she had bought Zane's novel. Perhaps as an act of contrition, a sort of peace gesture, she could apologize and ask him to sign it. Would he be pleased if she did so? Or merely scornful?

With a cold shock she realized suddenly that she was
staring at a copy of *her* last book, *My Pet Unicorn,* on the
shelf. She paled. There it was, marked down to half price,
crowded among a dozen or so other discounted children's
books. She picked it up, feeling slightly dazed by her dis-
covery.

She turned to the man, who was writing up her bill.

"What can you tell me about this?" she asked, holding
up the copy of *My Pet Unicorn.*

"Little," said the man, giving the book the most cursory
of glances. "I've heard it's inoffensive."

"Inoffensive?" Kelly asked, her voice rising. "What's
that mean?"

"By inoffensive, I mean precisely that—inoffensive," he
said, biting the words off curtly. "Bland. Not upsetting. A
sort of vanilla pudding of a book."

The blood rushed back to her cheeks. She put the book on
the counter beside Zane's. "I'll take this, too," she said almost defiantly. She didn't need another copy of her own
book, but she wanted to rescue it from the clutches of the
angular, acidic man.

She left the shop clutching a crisp bag, conscious that it
contained, in the form of the two books, a piece of her soul
and a piece of Zane's, as well. That their souls might never
be close in any other way gave her an odd wrench.

BACK AT JIMMIE'S, she was dismayed to find another vacation house had gained an inhabitant. This house was the
largest and most ornate on the lake and was not far from
Jimmie's. It resembled a Swiss chalet that had somehow
appeared in Arkansas and was now experiencing an iden-
tity crisis.

A shiny Lincoln Continental stood in the chalet's grassy
drive. A boat trailer was parked near the shore and a large,
sleek boat glittered as it bobbed, moored to the chalet's private dock.

From the chalet came recorded music—classical, but extremely loud. An opera soprano warbled shrilly. Kelly gritted her teeth as she got out of the car, cradling her sack of books.

"Yoo-hoo, Kelly," caroled Mavis Pruer from her deck, "how are you honey? I want to come over and introduce you to Dr. Hardesty. He got here right after you left."

Kelly could see Mavis's figure, shadowy behind the screened deck. The woman waved enthusiastically, and Kelly waved back, counterfeiting enthusiasm as best she could.

"Will you be there for a while?" called Mavis, raising her voice to be better heard above the music. "You're not going out again with your friend, are you?"

The pain in Kelly's chest tightened. "I'll be here."

She had time only to put away her few purchases, change her clothes and frisk a bit with Pollyanna, who had greeted her return with a joy usually reserved for welcoming home victorious armies.

Then Mavis was tapping relentlessly on the door. Kelly, dressed in a white shirt and white shorts, swung the door open to let her in. She swept up the dog in one arm to keep her from knocking Mavis over. The dog's tail beat wildly at the wonderful prospect of visitors. "I have to get to work," Kelly said, "but please come in for a minute."

"No, no, no," Mavis said. She was dressed in a flowered housedress and a white apron. "We're not coming in. Dr. Hardesty's still unloading and I have baking to do. Perhaps I'll be over later to bring you a little treat."

Mavis's eyes flashed conspiratorially and her mouth pursed in a way that seemed both coy and flirtatious. "And *this,*" she said with a significant nod, "is Dr. Terry Hardesty. Dr. Hardesty, this is Kelly Cordiner, Jimmie's niece from Cleveland."

Kelly's eyes met a pair of hazel ones framed by an expensive pair of wire-rimmed glasses. Terry Hardesty was a slender man, slightly taller than Kelly. He was perhaps forty years old, and his dark hair was voguishly cut.

He wore a crisply starched blue shirt tucked into his equally crisp white shorts, and he was so tanned that he looked as if he had just come from an intensive week at the tanning salon. He had the air of a man accustomed to being pleased with himself.

"Hel-*lo*," said Hardesty, beaming.

He had a lean face, bright eyed behind his glasses, with gaunt cheeks and a neatly trimmed pencil-thin mustache. For some reason he made Kelly think of a well-dressed and smoothly groomed rodent.

"Pleased to meet you," Kelly said with less than admirable sincerity. She reached through the opened screen door to shake his hand. It was damp.

"Pleased to meet *you*," he returned, still smiling and still holding her hand. "Mavis tells me you're both a teacher and a writer. We have something in common. I'm a psychologist."

Kelly wasn't sure what that gave them in common. She was glad when she managed to draw her hand away from his moist and clinging grasp. "Are you the one playing the music?" she asked. It still reverberated through the trees, shaking the quiet air.

"You can't have too much good music," Terry Hardesty said with a grin.

Kelly was about to disagree politely, but Mavis spoke. "Guess what, Kelly! Dr. Hardesty has a brand-new boat and he's invited us to go for a ride this evening. Isn't that wonderful? A lovely boat ride to explore the lake. Won't it be fun?"

"I—" Kelly began.

"I'll bring my tape player," Terry Hardesty interrupted, smiling smugly. "I'll play *Madama Butterfly*. I'll not only listen to the story of a beautiful woman, but I'll be *with* two beautiful women. Perhaps I'll bring a bottle of champagne, as well.''

"I don't think I—" Kelly started again.

Mavis's face took on a playful pout. "Kelly, don't you dare say no. If you don't go, I won't go. I just won't. And I *want* to. As little as I get around with this poor broken leg of mine—oh, it'll be like a party, the first one I can remember in ages. And with champagne! Real champagne! You *have* to go. I'll be so disappointed if you won't.''

"But—" Kelly said.

Dr. Hardesty performed a motion somewhere between a bow and a bob. "I won't take no for an answer," he said with a grin that made his cheeks seem skeletal.

"Oh, I think you had mail in your box," Mavis said. "Did you get it? Would you like me to bring yours when I get mine? I just live for mail. I'm always the first one to the mailboxes. I'd love to do it for you.''

"No, thanks," Kelly said, "I can get it myself." She had already picked up her one piece of mail, a blue envelope with her mother's familiar writing flowing across its surface. It lay, still unopened, on her desk.

"Suit yourself," Mavis said cheerfully. "Just trying to be neighborly." Then her friendly face crumpled in a wince of pain. "Oof," she said. "My leg. It gives me twinges of such *incredible* pain sometimes. Well, honey, you don't know how much it helps to have something to look forward to, like our party tonight. I declare, I feel almost festive—like a young girl again. Especially with our handsome Dr. Hardesty.''

Dr. Hardesty began to smile at the compliment, but his expression turned into one of mild alarm when Mavis flinched again, apparently in greater pain. "Ooh," she said, "I've overdone it, I'm afraid. Dr. Hardesty, would you help me back? I'd better rest—I don't want to miss our little cruise tonight. It'll be the highlight of my week!''

Terry Hardesty slipped his hand reassuringly under Mavis's elbow, then gave Kelly a smile that he must have intended to be rakish. He had rather prominent teeth, and for the second time she was reminded of a sleek rodent.

"We'll see you tonight," he said in a voice as smooth as silk. "Shall we say sevenish?"

"I'm not sure I—" Kelly started to say.

Once more Mavis Pruer cut her off. "Oh," she said, even though her voice was choked with pain, "I meant to give you these, dear. I thought you'd want them."

She put her hand in the pocket of her faded apron and drew out a packet of papers that looked like letters without envelopes. "They're from your uncle. He wrote so beautifully, you know. Just like you, I suppose!"

Kelly, surprised into silence, took the little stack of letters. They were folded up but written on the paper Jimmie always used. The pages were from a plain, old-fashioned writing tablet, white with blue lines. Such a tablet still sat on his desk.

"Oof!" Mavis said again, and acted as if she might have sunk to the ground in pain without the support of Dr. Hardesty. "Oh, I *am* having a spell. I have to go, honey. We'll see you tonight."

Leaning against Dr. Hardesty, Mavis made her way back to her own small house. The opera music reached some sort of crescendo and shook the very leaves on the trees. Kelly swung the door shut, grateful to deaden it, even if not completely.

"I don't dislike classical music," she said to Pollyanna as she set the dog on the floor. "I just don't like it so loud it knocks birds out of the sky." She and Dr. Hardesty were going to have to have a serious talk about decibels, the sooner the better.

She made sure all the windows were closed and then switched on the air conditioner to drown the sound out. She curled up on Jimmie's old green sofa and opened the envelope from her mother. It contained a card with a drawing of a sweet-faced rabbit on the front. Inside it said:

Hi, sweetheart,
You only just left, but I wanted to drop you a line, just so you'd have mail. I can't tell you how much I appreciate your taking on this job. You've always been the sweetest of daughters. Be *careful* down there.

Love, Mother

P.S.—be sure to make time to work on your book.

Kelly smiled at Cissie's thoughtfulness. *My book,* she mused, almost sadly. It seemed like days since she had thought about her book of fables. Perhaps she would dedicate it to Jimmie's memory. Yes, she thought, she'd like that and so would Cissie, and maybe, somewhere, so would Jimmie.

But the ache of sadness that had haunted her all morning remained, still knotting her chest. Kelly stared down moodily at the letters Mavis had given her from Jimmie. Idly she unfolded one and smiled at the familiar handwriting. It was true Jimmie wrote well, and he was his usual self in these letters, sometimes rueful, sometimes lyrical, sometimes funny.

He had written three letters to Mavis, rambling, friendly notes about the weather, the fishing, the scenery, his pets. Nothing in the first two surprised her. When she neared the end of the third one, however, what she read jolted her and made the knot in her chest harden until it weighed like a stone:

You remember the fishing pal I told you about—Zane? Well, Mavis, I've loved that man like a brother, but I swear I'm at the end of my rope.

He's got another girl in trouble. This time it's a little
schoolteacher over in Wayne County. Now, of course,
she wants to marry him, and of course he won't (as
usual).

I know this is no subject to discuss in a letter to a lady
like yourself, but as much as I like the man otherwise,
I'm about to end the friendship. He's fine to fish with,
but I start thinking about him getting near my niece or
a nice girl like her, and I can't stomach it. It's like the
man has a sickness in him.

I guess I will just break it off easylike and then ask
for my stuff back. I told you he was holding a few
things for me—things I mean for my sister and niece to
have. I might ask you to take them for me. They're just
some things I want kept safe and to go to them in case
anything happens to me. I know I can trust you, and
I'd rather they'd deal with you than him.

I saw one of the blue herons again today...

The letter went on, but Kelly could read no further. The
stone in her chest had grown jagged; it cut her so sharply
that tears stung her eyes. If Jimmie had lived, she thought
in confusion and grief, he would have severed his ties with
Zane altogether out of concern for her. Had he known he
was going to die, that she might soon meet Zane unless he
arranged otherwise?

Phrases of the letter slashed through her brain. "...an-
other girl in trouble...a schoolteacher...she wants to marry
him...he won't (as usual)...I can't stomach it...a sickness in him..."

Kelly folded up the pages, rose, went into the bedroom
and thrust the letters into an unused bureau drawer, slam-
ming it shut. She stared numbly into the mirror. Her face
was almost as white as her shirt, except for her cheekbones,
which bore thin flushes of hectic red.

She put her hands on the bureau to brace herself and looked away. There, on the nightstand, lay the thick book in its shiny black cover, *Her Demon Lover.*

Quickly she turned back and gazed into her own haunted eyes again in the mirror. Maybe, she told her image, Jimmie was wrong. It was totally unlike Jimmie to gossip, to speak ill of anyone, let alone commit such accusations to paper.

She shook her head, squeezing her eyes shut. But he had done it. The truth about Zane was clearly stated in Jimmie's familiar handwriting on Jimmie's familiar paper. Once more she remembered the tablet of it on his writing desk, the blue-lined paper he'd always used.

She threw herself onto the bed and hid her face in the pillow. Why should it hurt to find out that what Mavis had whispered was true? What did it matter? she nagged herself. So he was a better writer and a worse man than she had wanted to imagine—what difference did it make?

All the difference in the world, said some unhappy corner of her heart, *all the difference in the world.*

It was then she knew, as foolish as it was and as often as she'd been warned, she'd fallen a little bit in love with both the writer and the man.

If a little love hurt this much, she thought bitterly, she never wanted to experience it in greater quantity. Never. Cissie had been right.

CHAPTER EIGHT

ZANE HAD VOWED not to go near her again, at least not until his mind had regained its usual icy equilibrium and his blood had cooled down.

He hadn't meant to touch the woman again, especially when they had just said goodbye to Jimmie. But after all the solemnity, followed by that absurd dunking and all the helpless, liberating laughter, he had been unable to stop himself.

He was a man who took pride in the fact he never got swept away. Where his pride had vanished to for those few moments, he didn't know.

When she'd lain down beside him, one golden arm stretched over her head, her other hand clutching the damp white camisole, her wet hair fanned out against the stone, she had looked like a lean, beautiful mermaid.

Laughter had bubbled out of her, shaking the subtle curves of her breasts, and when she laughed, her face lit up like a star and she was dazzling. Normally his willpower was considerable, but willpower had dissolved beneath a surge of desire so strong that it had demanded he taste her lips and keep tasting them, touch her flesh and keep touching it.

Afterward she had frozen in disdain and regret, and he had wondered why in hell he had allowed himself to do such a fool thing. She was Jimmie's niece. She was just a kid. She'd seen too little of life, and he'd seen too much. He'd always been a loner, and after what had happened to his parents and then to him in Vietnam, he would always be one.

Besides, she had that condescending, holier-than-thou attitude about his work. It set his teeth on edge and did violent things to his usually even temper. He had thought that the years had hardened his hide against criticism, no matter how biting. But when the criticism had come so glibly from her pretty mouth, it had irked him to the marrow of his bones.

To shake her out of his system, he'd invited Annie Prudhomme, his neighbor's curvacious and red-headed divorced daughter, for an evening ride on the lake.

But Annie Prudhomme, who hung on his every word and kept leaning forward so he could appreciate her considerable cleavage, bored him. She kept raving that she wanted to read one of his books, because if he wrote the way he talked, why, goodness' gracious sakes alive, he must just write something *wonderful.*

What was he doing, he asked himself as he watched Annie artfully stroking her fiery hair against the ravages of the breeze. Here was eager, voluptuous Annie, and here he was, thinking about an uptight, too-tall, too-slender schoolteacher who, nose in the air, hated every sentence he wrote, even though she'd never bothered to read any.

He was almost glad when he recognized her on another boat across the lake. It was a big boat, a cabin cruiser, and she was standing with a man who seemed more than mildly interested in her. To compound the irony, the man was that idiot of a psychologist who usually turned up in the summer, the one Jimmie had aptly described as having about as much sense as a can of vegetable soup.

The two boats slowly passed each other, going in opposite directions, about thirty feet apart. Zane's lip curled in disgust. He'd never liked Hardesty and thought he was a crackpot.

Hardesty was cranky, self-absorbed and self-righteous. He held unshakable opinions on everything, opinions that Zane found idiotic and Jimmie had found hysterically funny. Hardesty was a pompous, self-loving bore who liked to boast of his accomplishments and romantic conquests.

Now Kelly stood by his side, her long legs golden against the white of her shorts, her chestnut hair streaming in the wind.

Hardesty talked to her animatedly and Kelly seemed to listen with great attention. She nodded and even smiled her beautiful smile at him.

Lord, thought Zane, was that the kind of man she wanted? The dogmatic, narrow-minded, yakking vegetable? Apparently she did, for she did not seem to notice Zane at all.

Hardesty was just the sort of twit she would like, Zane thought darkly. The two of them could spend hours congratulating themselves on their own superiority. They were both so repressed they probably deserved each other.

"I think the way you've made a living writing those little cowboy books is amazing," gushed Annie Prudhomme, gazing up into his eyes. "Why, if I had to think of enough words to write a whole book, my poor head would just bust. I'm just so terribly *impressed* I can't tell you."

"You're a dear girl, Annie," he said. Leaning forward, he kissed her on the nose. For some perverse reason, he hoped Kelly would see. He glanced back at her; she was still locked in conversation with Hardesty. She hadn't registered a flicker of reaction.

"Ooh," Annie cooed, "if you can kiss a nose that good, I wonder what you could do to a girl's *mouth.*"

If I can help it, my darling airhead, Zane thought wearily, *you'll never know.*

LOOK AT HIM, thought Kelly, watching avidly out of the corner of her eye. *Last night he was rolling around on the shore with me. Tonight he's kissing a redhead. What'll it be tomorrow? Two blondes with a brunette on the side for garnish?*

"Would you like to steer?" Terry Hardesty asked. He had changed his clothes for navy blue slacks and a perfectly ironed white shirt. His expertly barbered hair was concealed by a jaunty captain's cap, and he wore white deck shoes.

Kelly gave him a nervous smile. "I've never steered a boat in my life."

"Here," Terry said enthusiastically, "just take the wheel. I'll stand behind you—like this."

He maneuvered Kelly before the wheel, placing her hands on it. Then he snuggled behind her, putting his hands next to hers so that his arms were as good as around her, his chin nestling on her shoulder.

Revulsion quivered through Kelly, but she fought it back. She might as well be nice to him, she told herself. He had at least been kind enough to turn off his tape deck when she'd asked him to. He'd wanted to cruise up and down the lake, blasting out music. He said since *she* was the one who'd asked, he'd deny himself the pleasure.

"See?" Terry breathed against her neck. "You're quite the little first mate. Do you like being my 'mate'?"

He put suggestive emphasis on the word and Kelly shrugged haplessly, wishing he wouldn't cling so closely to her. He reeked of after-shave. His scent drowned that of the cool evening air and made her want to sneeze.

"Yoo-hoo," Mavis called from within the cabin, "who's ready for a brownie sundae with hot fudge? Is this the life or what, kids?"

"I suppose we ought to humor the old sweetie," Terry purred in Kelly's ear. "Isn't she a doll? Always so sweet to everybody."

Mavis was happily puttering in the boat's tiny kitchen.

Kelly nodded mechanically, staring after the other boat, which now shrank in the distance. If Zane had noticed her, he hadn't acknowledged it. He hadn't given her so much as a nod.

It was just as well, she thought bitterly. And that redhead of his had better be careful; Zane already had one woman pregnant, and apparently she wasn't the first. No wonder Jimmie was sick of the man.

But alone later that night as she lay in bed, finishing *Her Demon Lover,* she forgot her disdain—she was carried away by the book's emotional intensity. Reality faded to a vague blur, and she gave herself to the dark and fabulous world of Zane's creation.

When at last she read the book's final lines, she closed the cover and stared down at it for a long time. She ran her fingers over its glossy blackness, as if in a caress.

He was good, she thought in reluctant admiration. He was better than good. What a fascinating mind he had, what a potent imagination, what a strange power to weave a spell that was both sinister and beautiful.

Tonight she had been unable to put the book down. It was as if Zane had kidnapped her mind, ravishing it with the power of his own.

She visualized him—tall, slim hips and broad shoulders, straight brown hair streaked with gold, rugged

face and deep-set gray eyes. To a casual observer he
might seem to be only an uncomplicated outdoors-
man, interested in nothing more intricate than fishing
lures and fly rods.

It must be easy for him to pass himself off as the
writer of anonymous Westerns, a simple man writing
simple shoot-'em-ups. But he was not a simple man.
He was an extremely complex one, with a great and
eerie gift. He was an enchanter.

Enchanter, she thought, passing her fingertips again
over the book's dark cover. That, truly, was what he
was. And women should beware of enchanters. She
knew this well.

THE NEXT DAY Kelly fought the familiar struggle to
keep Zane from her thoughts. Although she yearned to
read his new book, *Illusions,* she did not allow herself
to do so. She kept it in its bag, tucked neatly in the bureau drawer beside the damning letters that Jimmie had
written. She forced herself to go about her business.

By the middle of the week, she had the house sparkling clean, the lawn cleared and was ready to get back
to her writing. She had no phone, and although she
missed not talking to Cissie, otherwise she didn't mind.
She loved living at the edge of the woods, looking out
at the lake and cliffs every day.

Mavis Pruer and Terry Hardesty, however, were not
the most ideal neighbors for a woman trying to write a
book. Mavis popped in two or three times a day, determined to chat. She showered Kelly with gifts of
food, from bowls of homemade soup to freshly baked
cookies.

Unfortunately Mavis had more enthusiasm for
cooking than she had talent, and Kelly usually put the
food away untouched. Once, although she felt guilty
doing so, she fed a bowl of Mavis's soup to Pollyanna

when she had run out of dog food. Pollyanna thanked
her with exuberant wags of the tail, but a strange look
came into her eyes when she began to lap it up.

"That bad, eh?" Kelly said sympathetically.

Kelly's only other contact with the outside world was
the mail. She'd had a letter from Cissie yesterday, saying she had hidden the key to the safety deposit box
and had just mailed in the signature form to the bank.
She asked once more if Kelly was sure such an ar-
rangement was safe.

Kelly shook her head in amusement at her mother's
fears. She was glad her mother had mailed in the form;
it must be safely in the bank's keeping now. She wrote
Cissie again, assuring her that the safety deposit box
was foolproof. Nobody, not even the bank officers
themselves, could get into the box without two keys,
the bank's and either of the ones Kelly and Cissie held,
and besides, there was the matter of matching the signatures.

Cissie's concern seemed a small problem to Kelly
compared with the growing irritation she felt over Terry
Hardesty. Kelly had quickly come to think of him as
unpleasantly eccentric and couldn't understand why
Mavis seemed so taken with him.

He apparently thought his degrees in psychology
gave him the right to evaluate Kelly's life and endlessly
attempt to improve it. He came calling frequently, although she'd never invited him over and neither had
she accepted any of his invitations. "I have to work,"
she would say.

"You're using your work as a defense mechanism,"
he'd respond. "It isn't healthy."

Today he had been particularly trying. He'd arrived
in the middle of the morning, bearing a pot of herbal
tea that he said would be better for her than her habit-
ual coffee.

Kelly sighed as she let him in. "I really shouldn't take a break," she said. "I have to work."

"How long are you going to hide from me behind this so-called work?" Terry asked, smiling as if he knew a secret that she didn't. Fussily he shooed the dog away from him.

Kelly bristled, but she poured tea for them, anyway. Anything, she told herself, to get him out as soon as possible. "I'm *not* hiding from you. You came here for a vacation. I didn't. I have work."

Terry, seated at the little kitchen table, eyed the house's interior with a critical eye. "Well, you've certainly cleaned up the mess. Your uncle's neurosis showed itself nowhere as clearly as in the way he kept this place. It was his way of rebelling against authority."

Kelly settled into her chair and gave Terry's bony face a disdainful glance. "My uncle wasn't neurotic. He wasn't rebelling against authority. He lived like a bachelor, that's all."

"Ah," Terry said. "You shouldn't think in generalities like that. *I'm* a bachelor. *I'm* also neat. Some people—insecure people—have even found me neat to a fault."

Kelly sighed. The only way Terry could be any tidier would be to wrap himself in cellophane. He had revealed he was divorced. She did not wonder why.

"And precisely what is it you write, little one?" he asked, leaning his chin on his hand. "You never say. I think today I'll stay until I find out."

Heaven forbid, thought Kelly. "I'm writing a book of animal fables."

A look of repugnance crossed his face. "Animal fables? You mean in which animals *talk* and so forth?"

"Yes," Kelly said, hoping she didn't sound as impatient as she felt. "They talk and so forth. What's wrong with that?"

"Well," Terry said, looking down his nose, "it invites the child to escape from reality. It's not wholesome."

"Fantasy is an important part of life," Kelly objected. "Children *love* fantasy."

"Children also love candy, even though it rots their teeth," Terry countered, taking a sip of tea. "You'd be better off writing about reality. For instance, you might write a book about a little boy whose sister always beats up on him because she's so viciously jealous. How he resolves this problem. I faced such a situation myself. Now *that* would be a helpful book. You're too bright to waste yourself on fantasy."

"I think fantasy is healthy," Kelly said, the set of her jaw grim.

"Take my advice," he countered. "You don't want to end up like that hack up the road. That what's-his-name. The cowboy writer."

"Zane?" Kelly said in disbelief. "Jimmie's friend?"

"Yes," Terry said with distaste. "And a good pair they made. Neither one capable of facing reality. Your uncle avoided it by drinking. The other one dwells in a world of clichés and false machismo. The gun, of course, is a sex symbol, so his fixation on guns and gunplay show that he's obviously insecure about his own—"

"Oh, really," Kelly said, her patience exhausted. "How can you sit there and talk about somebody you hardly know? And my uncle's drinking is not something I care to discuss."

"I understand your desire to repress thoughts about his flaws," Terry assured her. "But the point I'm trying to make is about fantasy."

Kelly's temper rose dangerously. "The best book I've read this summer was a fantasy. *Her Demon Lover,* by Farley Collins—"

"Oh, Farley *Collins,*" Terry said, frowning irritably. "Now the vogue for *that* man shows how unstable some of the public is. Writing about horror is infantile. There's a good deal of mystery about Farley Collins, but I can enlighten you. This man is reclusive because his life is dominated by irrational fears. My guess is that he was a sickly child with a weak father figure and a domineering mother. He's probably a hypochondriac and hides from the public because of his extreme insecurity. He's most certainly ridden with a great many phobias, and perhaps even fears leaving his own house—"

"That's nonsense," Kelly said irately, pushing her teacup away. "I've had enough. You don't know what you're talking about. I think you should leave."

Terry blinked in surprise, his dignity obviously wounded. "Kelly, don't be hostile. I'm trying to help."

"Then leave," she ordered. "And please don't interrupt me anymore. These are my *working hours.*" Her back rigid, she stood up, ready to show him the door.

He stood, too. His expression was patient, almost benign. "Kelly, think about what I've said. You'll see I'm right. Why don't we talk about it again tonight? We could go for another cruise around the lake."

"I don't want to go for a cruise. I'm going to work all day, then I'm going for a swim, then I'm going to write letters. I'm busy."

He frowned more irritably. "I've been meaning to speak to you about swimming when it gets dark. That's foolish. Mavis told me you do it, and I can't believe a woman of your obvious intelligence—"

"Terry, will you go away?" Kelly cried. "Will you just *go away?*"

"No need to get huffy," he said, in an obvious huff himself. "I'm leaving."

Kelly sighed with relief when she finally closed the door, shutting him out of her life. Pollyanna wagged more slowly than usual, apparently saddened that the company had gone.

Kelly put her hands on her hips and looked down at the dog, shaking her head. "I can't believe it. You *like* him. Only a saint or an idiot could like him."

She went back to her typewriter, hoping Terry hadn't infected her with a terminal case of writer's block. She always worked slowly, but lately her writing had gone at a dragging pace. She worried about it incessantly.

There were too many distractions, she rationalized. There had been all the work to do on Jimmie's house, there was Mavis, there was Terry, there was Zane—although Zane shouldn't be a distraction, because she hadn't seen him for days, even though she kept thinking about him. Oh, how she wished she would stop thinking about him.

There were other disturbing things, too. She had misplaced Jimmie's spare key. She had almost been sure it had hung on a nail by the door, yet now she couldn't find it. The loss perplexed her. What had she done with it?

So did other things. Usually, since she had come to Arkansas, her sleep had been uneasy, dream-haunted. But sometimes now she slept so deeply that she dreamed nothing at all. It was as if she fell into a bottomless pit of darkness that left her feeling strange and headachy in the morning.

Sometimes she had the irrational feeling that someone had been in the house, looking through her things. The papers on her desk would seem rearranged ever so slightly. The card from her mother temporarily disappeared, although she was certain she hadn't thrown it away, then just as mysteriously it reappeared.

She worried that she was imagining things and told herself she should never have read Zane's book. Beautiful as it was, its strangeness must have soaked into her, leaving her uneasy and paranoid.

In addition, she still had the formidable task of finding homes for three of the cats and for silly little Pollyanna. Pollyanna had scared her badly yesterday by getting sick, so sick that Kelly had almost driven her to the vet. Then the dog, showing a dog's amazing recuperative powers, seemed fine again. Kelly had been relieved and realized that she was becoming fond of the good-natured little thing.

No, she thought, staring at the sheet of paper in her typewriter, how could the work come easily when she had so much on her mind? Everything from the pets to the lost key to Zane. From outside she heard a sudden blast of music. To please her, Terry Hardesty had kept his music tuned low until today. Now, rebuffed, he was punishing her by turning it up full volume.

She knew objecting would do no good. He was doing it out of spite. She would have to close all the windows and turn on the air conditioner to block out his noise.

She wished Zane were there. Zane would go to Terry and demand the music be turned down. And if Terry didn't comply, Zane would pick him up by the scruff of his neck and fling him into the lake. Yes, Zane was forceful enough to deal with it quite handily.

Stop thinking about him, she scolded herself, feeling sick. *Stop thinking about him. You may never even see him again.*

EVENING FELL. Terry, thank heavens, had gone off to play on his boat, taking his everlasting music with him. Kelly, her back aching, rose from the typewriter and went into the bedroom to change into her swimsuit.

She had not taken time to eat, only nibbled a cupcake Mavis had brought her yesterday. It tasted dry and almost bitter. Mavis's baking had its ups and downs, and the cupcake, Kelly decided ruefully, was definitely a low point. But she forced it down.

She played a running game of tag on the shore with Pollyanna, for the dog had spent most of the day lying faithfully at her feet and needed the exercise. At last, almost breathless, her heart beating heavily, Kelly waded into the water, leaving Pollyanna sitting on the pebbles, staring wanly after her.

It was a lovely evening, for the sunset was particularly fiery, lighting the clouds with red and gold. The water was slightly cooler than the warm air, flowing like silk against her skin.

Kelly stroked easily toward the cliffs on the other side of the lake and played there, diving and swimming underwater. Tonight she found that she tired more quickly than usual. Her limbs felt unnaturally heavy.

She frowned, treading water and peering toward the opposite shore. How odd, she thought, her vision seemed somewhat blurry. She could see Pollyanna, a motionless white dot, waiting patiently for her return. For a moment the dot seemed bright and distinct, then it grew hazy.

Kelly narrowed her eyes. She realized suddenly that she didn't feel well. A wave of nausea rolled through her.

Oh, drat, she thought. She'd worked and worried and gone without eating until her body had rebelled. She pushed off from the cliff and started swimming toward home, using her most efficient stroke, a crawl.

She was almost midway between the two shores when
her stomach seared with a burning pain, then cramped
with such violence that she doubled up, gasping and
accidentally inhaling a mouthful of water.

She coughed and tried to straighten her body, to keep
on swimming. But another cramp bent her and her
strokes and kicks grew wild. The water choked her
again, ragged in her throat. She thrashed, struggling
for air, but could find only more mouthfuls of water.

A new pain stabbed through her, knotting her body
more helplessly than before. She opened her mouth to
cry out, and swallowed more water, which made her
gag, then wretch.

This can't happen, she thought in panic. *This is the
kind of thing that happens to other people. This can't
happen to me.*

She choked again, her mind dimming in sick panic
as she sank under the water again. *No,* she rebelled,
strangling as she inhaled still more water. But she
couldn't straighten her body, couldn't control it. *This
can't happen! No!*

But it was happening. She was helpless. She was
drowning.

THE ARMS AROUND HER were strong. Strong.

Her head hurt, her throat and lungs burned, her
stomach ached, her limbs were useless, she did not have
the strength to open her eyes.

But the arms that held her were strong. She was safe.
The arms were friends.

Kelly was vaguely conscious of being stretched facedown on something hard and prickly. Was it grass? She
wasn't sure. She was cold. She shuddered convul-
sively.

Powerful hands bore down painfully hard on her
back, making her gasp when they released their pres-

sure. Such large lungfuls of air burned, and she wanted only to rest, to drift back to the blackness.

But the hands pressed against her again, too hard, forcing her to take another painfully deep breath. The hands were her enemies. They would not let her alone; they tormented her until her breathing, aching and wheezing, was almost even.

The hands turned her on her back. They stroked her brow, wiped her face. Something else touched her face, something warm and damp: a dog, she thought groggily, a dog was licking her.

Then she was hoisted into the arms again and carried. Her own arms dangled helplessly and her eyelids seemed sealed with weakness. She felt herself being borne through the darkness and the journey seemed an infinitely long and painful one.

She heard a door shut. The arms carried her to a soft place and let her rest there. Bed. She was in bed. Now she could sink into the blackness and be safe.

No. Something slapped her cheek, stinging. She tried to turn her face away, but the slap came again.

Thunder growled. "Snap out of it. Come on."

The third slap stung harder, and tears singed her eyes. She opened them, painfully, trying to see her torturer.

A face swam before her, a worried face, a rugged face, a nice face.

A hand gripped her chin; an arm went around her, forcing her to sit up. "Come on," he said, staring into her eyes. "I know you're in there. Come back to me."

His deep eyes were gray, webbed like shattered glass. She knew those eyes. She had lost herself in them before and was finding herself in them now.

"Zane?" The word hurt her throat.

"The one and only."

She shivered so violently that her teeth rattled. He shifted her so that she sat on his lap, her head against his shoulder. "Settle down," he said. He was so warm and so strong that she wanted to lean against him forever.

She closed her eyes again, savoring his solidity. "Something happened."

"Obviously." His hands moved over her back, gentling her shudders away, soothing her.

"I got sick."

"I know. I'm one of the things you were sick on."

She moaned in humiliation.

He rubbed her back. "It's all right. Nothing a few million gallons of lake water couldn't wash out. I'm rinsed quite clean again, thank you."

"You're wet," she said, realizing it for the first time.

"Very observant."

She shivered again and put her arms around him, hungry for the feeling of his support. "Did you save me?"

"You might say that."

"How?" she asked, burrowing against his shoulder. "Where did you come from?"

"Rode over. Horse. Knocked. Nobody home. Saw the dog on the shore. Looked where it was looking. There you were."

"Was I—in trouble then?" She could not remember the sequence of events clearly. She pressed her face into his shoulder, rubbing her cheek against it.

"No. But you weren't swimming right. Not straight. Then you just—jackknifed."

"Thank you," she breathed. She could feel the steady beat of his heart. *You're safe,* its strong sound said in her ear. *You're safe. You're safe. You're safe.*

"Come on," he said softly. "I'm going to lay you down now, cover you up."

"No," she said. "Hold me."

He was silent. He ran one hand over her wet hair, smoothing it. She felt his heart beat harder.

"Hold me," she said again, "please. Please. Don't let go. Not yet."

A moment of silence hung in the air, broken only by the throb of his heart against her ear.

"All right," he said. He kissed her cheek. "All right."

He lay down with her in his arms.

"Just hold me," she begged, unashamed.

"Kelly, Kelly, Kelly," he said, his voice harsh and deep in his throat, as if he, too, were in pain. "I'll hold you. Yes."

CHAPTER NINE

KELLY AWOKE, feeling groggy, cold, achy and alone.

A quilt had been wrapped around her and a blade of light fell through the slightly open bedroom door. Pollyanna lay at her feet, staring up at her protectively and solemnly wagging her tail.

"Oh," Kelly moaned. She had risen on her elbow, but now fell back to the comfort of her pillow. She could not remember clearly what had happened, only sensed that something essential was missing, yet she could not pinpoint what it was that was gone.

"Did I hear a sign of life?"

She stiffened. Zane. That was what she missed so deeply. She had lain in his arms. Now he was gone from her. The bed seemed empty, desolate and deserted without him.

"I said, are you alive?"

She wrapped herself more tightly in the quilt. "I don't think so," she said.

The slant of light from the main room grew wider as he opened the door. "Too bad. I was just getting to like you."

She caught a glimpse of him, outlined in the doorway. She moaned again and turned away, laying facedown. She must look terrible, she thought. She put the pillow over her head.

He sat on the edge of the bed. "Why are you trying to hide?"

"I feel like something that should be hidden."

"That's a kid's trick. It doesn't work."

Gently he pried her fingers loose and took the pillow away. He stroked her tangled hair, smoothing it. "How do you feel?"

"Stupid," she muttered, her face against the sheet, her eyes squeezed shut. "Incredibly stupid." How wonderful the touch of his hand felt. How comforting it was to have him near again.

His fingers brushed the back of her neck, then closed over it, rubbing. "I mean physically."

"Cold. Wet. Achy. And stupid."

"Ah," he said, taking her by the shoulders and forcing her to turn over. She blinked, looking up at him. He was shadowy in the light that fell through the door, the planes of his face gilded. "You need a hot bath. And something hot in you. And a clean, dry bed. Let's see what we can do. Where's your robe? The one that covers every inch of your body and then some."

"In the closet," Kelly said with a sigh. His hand lay on her brow, resting.

"You don't have a fever," he said. "Come on. Upsy-daisy."

He lifted her to a sitting position and held her a moment longer than necessary. The moment was only a heartbeat long, but it filled Kelly with a strange, sweet yearning that burned through her with a lingering glow. She fought the desire to wind her arms around his neck and nuzzle against his chest. Suddenly she wished he could hold her forever, kiss her as he had that night on the shore.

But he released her and stood. "Do you have any idea what happened to you out there?" he asked. He went to her closet, drew out her robe and handed it to her.

She took it, her hand brushing his. She wished his merest touch didn't make such currents of desire shoot through her. "No. I just—cramped up. I've read about such things. It never happened to me before. It never happened to anybody I knew."

"But you're all right?" He reached down, grasping her shoulders again, pulling her to her feet, so she stood just a few inches from him. His hands fell away from her all too quickly.

She took a shuddery, deep breath. "I'm fine. Whatever it was is over."

"Good," he said. "Now hit the showers. I'll make you some eggs."

He put one hand on her shoulder and steered her toward the bathroom.

Kelly felt weak-kneed, and it was odd to undress, to be naked and vulnerable with a man so near. But the warmth of the water revived her and made her feel atingle with life again. She wrapped herself in the oversize robe, toweled her freshly washed hair and padded into the house's main area.

Zane stood at the range, stirring a frying panful of scrambled eggs. He gave her a mildly curious look, but said nothing.

He scraped the eggs onto a plate, deftly caught a piece of toast as it popped out of the toaster, and set eggs and toast on the table. "Sit," he ordered her. "Eat."

Kelly sat. "You'd make somebody a wonderful wife," she said. The eggs looked delicious, and somehow even the instant coffee steaming in the mug smelled better when he made it.

"Right," he muttered, sitting across from her. "I remade your bed, too. Next thing I'll be scrubbing your floors and getting housemaid's knee. But does anybody appreciate how I slave over a hot stove and work my fingers to the bone? No."

Kelly began eating the eggs with greedy satisfaction. She was ravenous. "I appreciate you. You saved my life and you can cook. How can I not appreciate you?"

He shrugged. "I'm sure you'll find a way."

"Listen," Kelly said, feeling warm and expansive and for once comfortable in his presence, "I owe you an apology. I read your book. *Her Demon Lover*. It's wonderful."

She expected some sort of reaction. She had thought he would be pleased or flattered or skeptical or seized with a fit of modesty. He merely leaned his chin on his fist. " 'Wonderful' is probably an understatement."

She was sorry she'd wasted the compliment on him and flashed him a daunting look. "Not conceited, are you?"

"I love it when you get your schoolteacher look. No. I'm not conceited. Sometimes when you do the work, you know you've got it right. That one, I knew."

Kelly sighed and took another sip of coffee. There was obviously no arguing with him. "All right," she said grudgingly. "I just wanted you to know. I misjudged you. I was wrong."

"Then why," he asked calmly, regarding her with cool gray eyes, "do I get the feeling you still disapprove of me? Good lord, you do get a schoolteachery look on your face. At two o'clock in the morning, too."

"Two o'clock?" Kelly cried. "It's two o'clock?"

"You slept for almost five hours. I stayed around to make sure you were all right. What's the matter? Afraid I've ruined your reputation?"

Kelly colored and stared into her coffee cup. "I just didn't know it was so late."

"Your neighbor came around, checking on you, wanting to know who I was. Mavis what's-her-face. She saw me carry you in. I don't like her. She's pushy. And there's something off-putting about her. Phony."

"She means well," Kelly said, still staring into her cup. She wondered if Mavis was watching even now, worried because Zane was with her. "She's just overly protective—because she's lonely or something."

"She doesn't strike me as lonely. She strikes me as hungry. I'm just not sure what she's hungry for. And she seemed uneasy about me—evasive, even. I also had words with your other neighbor. About his music. I told him to stifle it—you were asleep."

Kelly looked up, her eyes widening. "You and Terry? You had words?"

He shifted his shoulders restively. He gave her a look that was neither a frown nor a smile. "Look, Jimmie 'had words' with him last summer over his blasted music. The guy's a menace, a noise polluter. He may be your boyfriend, but—"

"He's not my boyfriend," Kelly interjected.

"Not to hear him tell it," Zane returned, and the gleam in his eyes was wicked. "He followed me back over here, insisting he was going to be the one to take care of you. He said, and I believe this was his exact term, that you were his 'property.'"

"His *property?*" Kelly exclaimed. "How dare he say such a thing? I'm nobody's *property.*"

Zane laughed. It was not a pleasant laugh. "You'll have to work that out with him. You looked like his property the other night on his boat. At any rate, I sort of threw him off your porch. I hope it doesn't do permanent damage to your relationship."

Kelly raked a hand through her damp hair in frustration. "Threw him off my porch? You actually threw him?"

"Yes," Zane said icily. "He got on my nerves. So I picked him up by his collar and the belt of his fancy boating pants and I pitched him over the railing. It's all right. He landed on his feet."

She looked at him, not knowing if she should be pleased or appalled. Zane was such a large man he probably could have thrown someone far larger than Terry Hardesty over the railing and thrown him hard. She tried to look disapproving. "Violence isn't the solution to anything," she said primly, although earlier she had wished Zane would throw Terry in the lake.

He gave her a dark and humorless stare. "Did you ever try to talk sense to that jerk?" he demanded.

"Yes."

"Trust me. Violence is the only solution."

She almost smiled. Terry was impossible, of course; he was opinionated, pigheaded and spiteful, and probably the only way to make a point with him was to treat him exactly as Zane had done.

She shook her head and clutched the collar of her robe, pulling it more tightly shut. "You're very misanthropic tonight. You don't like anybody."

"No," he agreed, meeting her gaze with his own disconcertingly steady one. "And I'm not happy with you, either. I told you not to swim alone."

Kelly pushed her empty plate away. What had happened to her was freakish, inexplicable, a once-in-a-lifetime anomaly. But both Zane and Terry had warned her. She was suddenly tired of men telling her what she should and shouldn't do. She said nothing, only set her chin more stubbornly.

"If I hadn't come along, you'd be fish food," he muttered. "What a stupid waste."

"All right, all right," she agreed wearily, waving her hand in a gesture of dismissal. "I won't do it again. I'm lucky you turned up to save me from my own folly, et cetera, et cetera, blah, blah, blah." She put her face in her hands, suddenly feeling frightened and ashamed and shaky again. "Why did you come along, anyway? Or did you think you'd just drift over this way just to look down your nose at all of us?"

He said nothing for a long moment. She rubbed her eyes, which smarted with unshed tears. She had been both terribly unlucky and lucky in the same night. It left her feeling drained and confused.

She kept her hands clamped against her face because it was easier to shut Zane out than look at him. It cost her too many emotions to look at him. As always, he made a storm of feelings rise in her, pulling her first this way, then that.

Why did she feel so strongly attracted to him, when she knew what kind of man he was? Jimmie's damning letter was in the next room, describing in detail just how irresponsible Zane was. And Mavis, watchful Mavis, had told her repeatedly, and Mavis had no reason to lie.

"I wanted to talk to you," he said at last, his voice harsh.

"Then talk," Kelly said, her voice muffled. "What did you want to talk about?"

"Look," he almost growled, "are you going to cry again?"

"No," she insisted, but she heard the tremor in her voice and hated it.

"I'll tell you later," he said in the same impatient tone. "It can wait. You're going to do it, aren't you? You're going to cry. Don't."

"I'm *not* going to cry, and I will if I want to," Kelly said illogically, the lump in her throat making her choke the words out.

"Go to bed," he ordered, no sympathy in his voice. "Go on. Just get to bed."

She shook her head, keeping her face covered.

"I'm going," he said. "I can't do you any more good. Just go to bed."

She nodded numbly. She heard the scrape of his chair as he stood. She sensed that he stood there a long time, just staring down at her. He said nothing. He exhaled sharply, then the heel of his boot squealed slightly as he turned to leave. She heard his long steps crossing the room, the door opening and then closing behind him.

When she was alone at last, she allowed herself to cry. She remembered being amazed and terrified when she realized she might drown. Somehow Zane, strong, wonderful Zane, had saved her. But she also remembered Jimmie's letter and all the women that Zane had possessed and wronged, and she wept bitterly. It had been sweet to be in his arms, all too sweet, and like a fool she had loved it.

ZANE RODE AWAY in the moonlight, watching the way the shadows played and moved in its silvery glow.

He'd left her so abruptly because he couldn't stay in that little house any longer without taking her in his arms again, and he knew this time if he held her, it would not be to comfort her into the ease of sleep.

He wanted to make love to her until the stars shook out of the heavens. And that was stupid, because most of the time she acted as if he were some sort of moral leper. Yet, maddeningly, at other times she looked at him with a softness in her eyes that made him want to take her in his arms and never let her go. It made no sense. What could he, a man determined to live a quiet and sensible life, want with such a bundle of contradictions?

He shouldn't want her at all. She was too young, she was wrong for him in a thousand different ways, she disapproved of him for reasons he couldn't begin to understand; and there was something else besides. He had something to tell her. When he did, he would hurt her, badly and deeply. She wouldn't want him near her again, let alone in her bed. But he had to tell her, as an honorable man.

The gray horse moved on, bearing him away from her through a world of shifting shadows.

KELLY AWOKE to Mavis's persistent tapping at the door. Groggily she swept her hair away from her face and pulled on her robe. The dog danced excitedly about her as she made her way to the door.

"You poor *dear*," Mavis said when she saw Kelly. "Are you all right? What time did that man leave? I tried to get in to take care of you, but he was cross as a bear with a sore head. Are you *sure* you're all right?"

"I'm fine," Kelly assured her, although emotionally she felt far from fine and she was in no mood to let Mavis play mother hen.

"Well, you *look* terrible," Mavis said helpfully. "I woke you up, didn't I? Go scoot into the bathroom, fix yourself up and I'll make you a good breakfast. I want to see some meat on those bones."

Kelly insisted she didn't want breakfast and she didn't want Mavis going to any trouble. Mavis finally settled for making the coffee, and Kelly, sighing with frustration, went to wash her face and brush out her hair.

She returned, and Mavis bustled and fussed, making her drink the coffee, asking her half a hundred unrelated questions.

Had Kelly gone swimming after eating? Didn't she know that was dangerous? Was she getting enough rest? She looked like someone who needed a straight month of sleep. Had she heard from her mother lately? How was dear Cissie? Did that awful Graye man try to put a move on her?

Mavis really *didn't* want to gossip, but Jimmie had said a girl had tried to kill herself over that Graye man, and Mavis would feel she had failed both Jimmie and Cissie if she stood by and let Kelly get involved with a man like that.

Kelly suddenly felt ill again, dizzy and sick and so tired that she wanted to crawl back into bed and sleep for several million years. If she could only rest, her mind would clear. She would stop thinking of Zane and losing things and imagining phantoms went through her house by night.

When she told Mavis she didn't feel well, Mavis actually wanted to tuck her into bed and stay by her side. Kelly, exhausted, had to beg her to leave.

She crept back to the bedroom and was going to get back into bed, when a blast of classical music broke the still air. She peered between the blinds and saw Terry Hardesty sitting on his porch, his tape deck booming.

He was wearing swimming trunks and had oiled his skinny body until it gleamed. He appeared to have his attention glued to a thick book, but from time to time he glared pointedly at Kelly's house, as if he were giving it—and her—the evil eye.

She sighed, climbed into bed again and managed to sleep uneasily in spite of Terry and the crashing strains of Beethoven.

She awoke again to someone knocking on her door. It was not an insistent, peppery knock like Mavis's or a self-important, annoying one like Terry's. No, this knock was impatient and authoritative and she recognized it at once: it was Zane's.

Painfully she rose from the bed and made her way to the door. She tried to smooth her tumbled hair, to straighten the robe she had not even bothered to take off.

Opening the door, she winced against the assault of the sunlight. Zane stood framed by a dazzle of light so bright he seemed like a man made of shadows. Behind him she saw a glistening dark Jeep. He had so many ways to arrive, she thought in confusion. He was always transporting himself by a different mode, like a wizard.

"You're still asleep?" he asked in disbelief. "Are you sick again or what?"

Kelly furrowed her brow in confusion. "I'm fine. I guess I was just exhausted. Come in."

He stepped inside and looked down at her with a mixture of anger and concern. "It's past noon. Have you slept all this time?"

Her head ached, but otherwise her body felt almost normal. It was Zane who unsettled her. He wore stone-colored jeans and a dark blue shirt that made his hair seem almost blond, his eyes almost blue.

"I got up and had coffee with Mavis," she said, rubbing her forehead.

"Have you eaten?" he demanded.

She shook her head. "I only slept. I'm surprised I could. Terry was out there with his tape deck going full-blast, looking over here as if he were putting a curse on the place. He's starting to make me nervous. He's *odd*."

He nodded, his eyes roaming from the top of her head to her feet and back again. "I saw him. When he saw me, he turned it down and scuttled inside. The little lady next door was about to descend on him. She was carrying him a plate of something."

Kelly looked away, uncomfortable under his scrutiny. "She's always baking things for people, always bringing me something. I wish she wouldn't. She's just lonely."

"Maybe. But I swear there's something about her I don't trust."

She feels the same about you, Kelly wanted to snap, but didn't. She shook her head again, still feeling dazed. She glanced warily at Zane. He stood, one hip cocked, his arms crossed, one shoulder held higher than the other.

"You came back," she said softly. "Why?"

He set his jaw so that its line was harsh. "To see how you were. And talk. But first, get dressed. I'm tired of that bathrobe. It looks like you could wrap up Rhode Island in it."

She gave him a wan smile. Ten minutes later she felt better, with her hair brushed until it gleamed and fresh clothes on—white slacks, a pale pink shirt and white sandals.

He was at the stove again, turning over a batch of very credible-looking silver-dollar pancakes.

"Why are you being so domestic?" she asked warily, standing with her back to the refrigerator. "Won't it ruin your image as the king of thrillers?"

"I stay invisible so I don't have to worry about an image. I like privacy. And I couldn't find anything else to feed you. Your refrigerator is full of old cookies and cupcakes that look like rocks."

"Mavis," Kelly said with a sigh. "She tries so hard. I hate to hurt her feelings." Turning, she opened the refrigerator door and took out the platter that held Mavis's hardened offerings. She put them in a sack and set it on the counter. "Take these home with you. Feed them to your chickens or whatever. I feel guilty just throwing them out. And Pollyanna's picky. She won't touch them."

Poor Mavis, Kelly thought, moving to the deck and staring out at the water. The woman wanted to be creative in the kitchen, but usually her efforts were merely pathetic. It was sad, for Mavis tried so hard to please.

Zane joined her on the deck, setting a plate of pancakes and a container of syrup on the little table that overlooked the lake. "Sit. Eat," he said.

Kelly turned to him. "You're always telling me to sit and eat," she said. A breeze rose, fluttering his streaked hair.

"Right," he said without smiling. "Sit. Eat."

She sat. He brought her silverware and a cup of coffee, then sat across from her. As usual his deep-set eyes were trained on her, making her uneasy and self-conscious.

"Why are you always feeding me?" she asked. "And watching me like that?"

"I feed you because you need feeding. I watch you be-cause—" he gave a rasping sigh "—because I'm a watcher, that's all."

He turned away, staring moodily out at the cliffs. Kelly ate in silence, and she, too, kept her eyes on the lake, the cliffs. It was as if the two of them had run out of things to say.

"Thank you," she said at last. She thought again of all his women and wondered how he could be so cruel and yet so kind. Perhaps this was his pattern; first he was kind. The cruelty, the coldness, came later. "It was delicious. But you don't have to keep this up. You don't have to baby-sit me."

"I know," he said curtly, still not looking at her. The breeze shifted, catching and lifting the forelock of his hair. Another awkward silence hung between them. "That woman," he said at last, his voice thoughtful. "Mavis. I remember Jim talking about her—a little. She kept writing him. He wrote her back a couple of times, but he didn't like her much. I think she may have got him drunk, and maybe he said something he shouldn't have. He wouldn't talk about it much. It was as if she worried him, and he didn't know quite why. Now she worries me." He shook his head.

Kelly frowned, waiting for him to say more, but he didn't. She could hardly imagine sweet-faced little Mavis getting anyone drunk. "That can't be true," she said. "It's just a product of your weird imagination. The two of them were friends. He trusted her—quite a bit."

He trusted her more than he did you, she wished she could say. *You ruined his faith in you—and for good reason. Did you know he was going to turn to her instead of you? Is that why you dislike her? Because you knew?*

He turned his cool and steady gaze on her. "I said he didn't care for her. He was one of my best friends. I ought to know."

He didn't want to be your friend any longer, Kelly thought bitterly. *He was tired of your ways. He couldn't respect you.*

"It just so happens I saw the letters he wrote her," she said, her back straight and her shoulders squared. "I *have* the letters he wrote her. He obviously thought very highly of her. He—he confided in her."

Zane gave the short, mocking laugh of which he was the master. "Look, I'm not going to fight about her. We have more important things to fight about."

She tensed, not liking the way his face had hardened. "Fight? What about?"

He took a deep breath and exhaled it sharply. "Your books. What you've written. And your fables. What you're writing now."

A pang stabbed her. "Oh," she said as calmly as she could. "You read my books. And you don't like them.

Well—I didn't expect you to. We look at things too differently."

"That's not it," he said, shifting his shoulders impatiently. "Look, I wouldn't bother if you weren't Jim's niece. I hide from aspiring writers as if they carry the plague. I don't read their stuff, I don't give advice and I don't try to teach. But I'm afraid in your case, as usual, I've got to make an exception."

Her face grew hot. She ran her hand nervously through her long hair. "They're not *that* bad," she said defensively. "They got published, didn't they? And my agent's seen part of the fable book. She says she can sell it. So just because you don't—"

"Kelly, I'm sorry. It's why I came to talk to you last night, but last night obviously wasn't the time." His voice was so gruff it sounded cruel, cutting. "Your books are all right, but only all right. You—cheat when you write. And if you don't stop, you'll never be as good as you could be. You'll just be ordinary—no more."

"Cheat?" she said with a gasp of hurt. "Cheat?"

"Cheat," he repeated grimly. "You're not honest. You make everything too pretty, too goody-goody. You don't want to admit there's evil in the world. You don't want to look at it. You don't even write about real animals, for God's sake. Unicorns, teddy bears...why can't you let yourself go—write about something you really feel strongly about—not just imaginary things?"

She was stunned, wounded, betrayed and humiliated. She had been kind about his work, almost gushed over it. Why was he being so cruel to her? She clutched at the edge of the table so tightly that her knuckles whitened. "You don't know anything about children's books—"

"I know about writing," he almost snarled. "I know when it rings true. And I know that every great kid's story has a dark side—a witch, a wizard, a wolf, a troll, a curse, a threat. Kids *want* to deal with that dark side—they need it. It's one of the ways they grow up.''

"All right," Kelly said, hurt and furious. "You've made it clear. I'm shallow and dishonest. And maybe I did hold back too much on the first two books. But the fables are different. I'm much more in control of the fables. They're going to be—"

He cut her off, slashing the air with a fierce, impatient motion. "The fables *aren't* any different. You're in too much control—you're strangling the life out of them."

"How do you know?" she challenged hotly. "You never read them. I've never shown them to anybody except my agent. Not even my mother—"

She stopped, aghast. She realized what he had done, and it dazed her as much as a physical blow. The blood fled from her face and she stared at him with shocked resentment.

"You read them," she accused, feeling violated. "Didn't you? Last night when I was asleep. You found my personal papers and *read* them—you had no right!"

"No," he said from between clenched teeth. "I didn't. But I wanted to know if you were making the same mistake again, so I could try to stop you. You are. You're doing it."

Kelly stood up so fast she almost upset the table. The plate slid off and crashed to pieces on the floor of the deck, but she hardly noticed. Zane rose, too, and the two of them stood glaring at each other like two fighters ready to spring.

"You had no right!" she repeated furiously. "I ought to—I ought to fling that coffee cup right at your head. You *beast*.''

"Fling away if it makes you feel better," he muttered. "The question is will it make you write any better? That's all I care about."

"How can I write any better?" she snapped sarcastically. "According to you, I've got no depth, no emotion, no talent, no courage. I'm nothing compared with *you*. I haven't got it in me to be a big, important, bestselling writer like *you*.''

A forked vein flickered at his temple like a small blue bolt of lightning. ''You have depth, you have emotion, you have talent—use them. Have you really looked at those fables? You're using imaginary animals again—another unicorn. A horse with wings. A toy dog that wants to be real. A sea serpent.''

''What's wrong with that?'' she cried, clenching her fists. ''Nothing's wrong with that! Nothing!''

''What's wrong with real animals and real emotions?'' he countered. ''What's wrong with writing about—about that dog, for instance? That goofy, worthless, love-crazy dog that nobody wants to love back?''

He gestured in disgust toward the dog, which stood, looking up bewildered at the two of them, wagging her tail sadly.

''I'll write what I want and how I want,'' Kelly raged. ''You're as bad as Terry, telling me how to do my job, what I ought to think and how I ought to think it and how I ought to live my life. And I'll tell you what I told him. Get out. Get out and don't ever come back again.''

''There,'' he said in angry satisfaction, pointing at her. ''That's passion. Why don't you try for once in your life to get that into a story?''

''Get out!'' she ordered. ''Get out before I do throw things at you. I mean it.''

''If you think it was fun doing this, you're wrong,'' he sneered. ''I could have just kept my mouth shut and let you do a mediocre job when you could do a great one. I wouldn't have said anything if I didn't think you could do it. Jimmie was my friend and I...''

Kelly's patience exploded like a firecracker whose fuse has burned to the powder. ''He wasn't your friend—he didn't even *like* you,'' she flung at him. ''You made him sick, you and your ways. He'd had enough of you.''

Zane frowned, obviously taken back by her venom. "What?"

"He wasn't your friend and he knew exactly what sort of—of monster you are," Kelly said, her eyes narrowed murderously. "He despised you. And I can prove it." She stalked to the bedroom and slammed through the bureau drawers until she found the letters. She marched back into the main room. Zane stood in the kitchen area, his face stormy, his posture dangerous.

"Here," Kelly said, jamming the letters into the same bag with Mavis's cookies. "They're where they belong. With the other garbage. Go through the garbage to see for yourself what he really thought of you—you scum. 'Scum' is too kind a word. No wonder you write about monsters—you're one yourself. And now, *go.*"

She thrust the bag into his hands, strode to the front door and flung it open. "Out," she ordered. "Now."

He stalked past her, then stopped, turned and took two steps toward her so he towered over her. The vein in his forehead flickered again and his gray eyes looked hard as diamonds.

"Write your fantasies, Kelly," he said, his voice a low hiss of anger. "But put some real feeling in them so people believe them. And remember that although there's a lot of good in the world, there's evil, too. Real evil. You can't ignore it. Not forever you can't."

"You've taught me that," she said bitterly. "You've taught me too well. You and my father both. Now—for the last time—get out."

He looked at her a long time, a mirthless smile forming crookedly at the corner of his mouth. "Goodbye," he said. Infinite contempt was in his voice. He turned and walked away.

Kelly slammed the door and walked dazedly to the couch. She threw herself on it, clutching a sofa pillow. She heard his Jeep pulling away, heard the sound of its motor fading in the distance.

She clasped one hand to her forehead, which was hot, almost feverish. She wanted to cry but had the sick, empty feeling that she'd used up all her tears, all her feelings, and that nothing was left.

After a few moments she rose dully and sat at Jimmie's desk, where her typewriter rested. She looked at her papers spread about. Yes, she could see he had meddled with them, even with her mother's latest letter, which had been refolded wrong. Had he even read her mail? she thought in disgust. What sort of vermin was he? She couldn't hate him enough.

But neither could she stop herself from picking up her half-finished manuscript. Unhappily she began to reread it, trying to imagine how it looked to his expert eyes, trying to see it as it was, rather than as how she wished it.

At least she could try to concentrate. Terry Hardesty's music had ceased. Perhaps Mavis had talked sense into him somehow. Quiet was welcome after so much turmoil.

But as Kelly read, the sickness and emptiness grew within her, and she found her hands were shaking. She skimmed through the first of her little animal stories, then the second.

Oh, no, she thought, shaking her head, *oh, no, no, no.* The stories were sweet, they were smoothly written, they were competent and cheery. But he was right. There was a peculiar emptiness at their center, a lack of anything that really mattered. The stories were mellow and bland and harmless. They were sterile.

When she heard Mavis's peculiar scuttling knock on the door, she could not bring herself to answer it. She sat, numbed and unhappy, rereading the fables. Her carefully wrought, carefully sanitized fables, in which no real danger ever threatened and nothing truly important was ever at stake. "Inoffensive," the man at the bookstore had called her other book. And that was the best that could be said for these stories. Inoffensive.

The past few weeks of Kelly's life had been complex, filled with emotion, almost too rich with it. But none of that emotion had found its way into her stories. She had protected herself from reality the same way she wanted to protect her readers. Zane had seen it immediately. She hadn't fooled him, but she had fooled herself badly and the shame of it made her head ache even more.

The irony seethed within her, churning her stomach. Zane was a despicable man but a good critic. It was the man, dangerous as he was, whom she was drawn to. It was the critic, the part of him that could help her, whom she feared and resented. Nothing made sense anymore.

"Kelly? Kelly, are you in there? Honey, are you all right? Was that awful man bothering you again? Let me in, sweetie."

"I can't talk," Kelly called out in a choked voice. "I'm fine. I can't talk, Mavis. Please—I need to be alone."

"Oh, honey, honey, I'm so worried about you—I've baked you some peanut butter cookies. Please let me in— I'm so *worried* about you."

"Later," Kelly managed to say, leaning her hot forehead against her hand. The words of her story blurred before her eyes, but she forced herself to shut the rest of the world out, to keep reading.

At last Mavis left, vowing to be back later, swearing she would take care of Kelly, that she felt it her duty.

Doggedly Kelly read her manuscript through, then forced herself to read it again. At last she set the stack of papers on the desk and stared at them as if seeing them for the first time. Tears of frustration pricked her eyes. Finally, with a feeling of infinite loss, she picked them up, tore them gently in half and dropped them quietly into the wastebasket.

She looked at Pollyanna, who stood watching happily, wagging her tail so hard that her hips swung from side to side.

Kelly swallowed hard. "We're starting over," she said. "Don't look so happy about it. It's going to be hard. Harder than anything I've ever done."

She cursed Zane with all her heart. But she would show him, she vowed. She would show him if it killed her. She sat at the typewriter like one possessed and put in a fresh sheet of paper.

Oddly, the words came more easily than they had all summer, now with her emotions roiling so closely to the surface. She wrote until darkness fell.

Mavis returned periodically, knocking and demanding to be let in. Kelly apologized through the closed door and said she couldn't stop working. She knew it was rude, but she was a person under a spell. She couldn't stop writing. Not now.

Mavis, undaunted, came back again after dark, saying she was leaving a plate of cookies on the doorstep. She wouldn't bother Kelly, but would Kelly please come get them when Mavis left? Mavis would hate to think of wild animals coming to eat them.

"Yes," Kelly called, feeling hard-hearted but too driven to care as she heard the soft clink of a plate being set on the step. Then she went back to her writing.

When she was sure Mavis was gone, she opened the door. The chipped blue-and-white plate of cookies sat there, a mute gift, and Kelly guiltily took them in, sorry she had been so inhospitable to Mavis.

She hadn't eaten since Zane had made her the pancakes. She nibbled two of the cookies and drank a glass of milk. Then, sleepy, she reluctantly covered her typewriter and stumbled off to bed.

Sometime during the night, she thought she heard the rattling rumble of a car's engine. Briefly she wondered if

Zane had returned, and the thought sent a wild mixture of emotions coursing through her. She was half grateful, half disappointed when she recognized the sound as the clanking engine of Mavis's blue compact.

Kelly glanced at the clock, but her vision was too blurred to read it. She knew only that it was late. Where was Mavis going at this time of night? Probably to a grocery store that was open twenty-four hours so that she could buy more baking powder and flour, Kelly thought groggily. But then she thought of Mavis no more. Sleep, dreamless and irresistible, claimed her again.

SHE WAS AWAKENED at six o'clock in the morning. Terry Hardesty was playing his tape deck full blast. Oh, Kelly thought miserably, he was an impossible, spiteful, childish man. What did he intend to do? Punish her for the rest of the summer? What other torments would he hatch? She had no idea. She was growing frightened of him.

Then, early as it was, someone began banging on her door. Her head felt fuzzy and heavy, and the whole world seemed insane.

She was dismayed to recognize the insistent knocking as Zane's. "Let me in," he demanded. "Let me in or I'll kick the door down, Kelly. You've got trouble."

She heard Terry Hardesty's petulant voice echoing through the morning. "Stop that shouting and banging! I'll report the two of you for disturbing the peace! And another thing, those nasty cats keep coming on my lawn, chasing birds from my bird feeder. I won't have it! I'll poison the beasts. I will—I'll fill them full of arsenic!"

"Hardesty," Zane's voice thundered, "if you don't let this woman—and these cats—alone, I'll personally force-feed you fifteen pounds of kitty litter—used. Kelly, open up, damn it! Are you in there? Are you all right?"

He gave the door a resounding kick. Kelly could hear it shake even in the bedroom. She rose and hurried to the front room, wondering if she would ever be at peace again.

"Don't you threaten me," cried Terry Hardesty. "You've already assaulted me once, and you'll hear from my attorney. You're a homicidal maniac. Stop kicking that door. That's breaking and entering!"

Zane kicked the door again, violently. Kelly swung it open, glaring. He looked at her with a kind of wild determination in his eyes and grimness in the line of his mouth. "You're all right?"

"No," she retorted, "I'm not all right. Terry's been playing music since dawn, and I've got two crazy men yelling threats at each other. You *kicked* my door. Terry's right—you're a maniac. What's come over everybody? What are you trying to do?"

"Send you back to Cleveland."

"What?" she demanded. "I can't. I have work to do. I have this house to sell."

His mouth was more stubborn than before and he was breathing hard. "No, you don't. I'll buy the house. I can afford it. It'll be a pleasure. So *you'll* go home. You're too much trouble. Pack."

He looked so fiercely unwavering that Kelly stepped back from him. "No," she said in defiance. "You don't give me orders. I won't pack."

"Yes, you will," he said, in a voice that half-frightened her and with a smile that sent a chill rippling up her spine. "You'll pack and I'll help. You're leaving, lady. No buts about it."

He picked her up in his arms and carried her, kicking and protesting, into the bedroom.

CHAPTER TEN

"PUT ME DOWN!" Kelly cried, hitting him as hard as she could in the shoulder with her fist. He didn't flinch, and all she accomplished was hurting her knuckles. She didn't care. She hit him again.

He dumped her unceremoniously on the bed, opened her closet and pulled out her suitcases. "You're leaving. You're a one-woman disaster area, and I'm sending you home. You and your mother can sit and read fairy tales together. I haven't got the time for all this."

He pulled open her dresser drawers and began throwing her things into the suitcases. When he got to her lingerie, he threw it in with more vehemence than anything else.

"Get your hands off my clothes!"

He hardly glanced at her and when he did his look was full of both ice and fire. "Did you see Mavis after I left yesterday afternoon?"

"No," Kelly said, rising from the bed. "And what business is it of yours?"

She began pulling her jumbled clothes out of the largest suitcase. He turned, grasped her by the upper arms and leaned over. His vehemence surprised and alarmed her.

"Did you eat anything she made for you?" he demanded.

"No," Kelly protested, conscious of the heat of his hands against her flesh. "Yes—a few cookies—why? What are you doing? *Stop* this!"

"Where's Mavis?" he asked, pulling her closer to him. "Where's she gone? It's only six-thirty, but her car's gone and her house is shut up like she's abandoned it."

"I don't know where she is," Kelly protested angrily. "Are you insane? What's this all about?"

He bent closer to her, his jaw set like granite. "I woke up early this morning to go fishing. In part, to forget about *you.* I found six dead chickens in the yard and one feeling mighty poorly."

"What?" Kelly demanded, trying to shake herself from his grasp. He made no sense and he was frightening her. She struggled harder to escape.

He shook her slightly to quiet her. He spoke through clenched teeth. "They were poisoned. I fed them that damned stuff Mavis gave you, and it poisoned them. She was drugging you. That's probably why you doubled up in the lake and nearly died."

"What?" she repeated, not comprehending. "What?"

Stunned, she no longer fought him. As senseless as his words sounded, they made terrible sense. Suddenly, random events took on a terrifying pattern. She remembered eating the cupcake before she went in the water.

With horror, she remembered how sometimes she slept so soundly it was as if she had been drugged, and there had been Mavis, always Mavis, on her doorstep, offering her something more to eat. With shock, she remembered feeding the soup to Pollyanna, and that was when the dog had gotten so sick. And since then, Pollyanna had refused to eat anything Mavis had cooked.

Kelly had slept as one dead after Mavis had made her coffee yesterday morning. And she had eaten the cookies last night and slept again, even though she had wanted to work.

She was rigid in Zane's grasp, staring at him, aghast. "She couldn't have," she said, shaking her head. "Why? Why would she drug me?"

His face remained just as relentless, his grip on her arms just as tight. "You had something she wanted. The jewels. Jimmie must have told her about them—he was likely drunk at the time. He probably told her more than he told any other women because she seemed so sweet and harmless and respectable."

Kelly wished he wouldn't glare at her so savagely or hold her so tightly. "But she can't get the jewels," she objected. "They're in the safety deposit box."

"No, they're not," he retorted. "Listen, I've lived in these hills a long time and I know a lot of people. I'm a quiet man, but I'll raise hell if I have to. I called the president of the bank at six o'clock this morning and made him check it out."

"Check what out?" Kelly asked numbly.

The muscles of his jaw were taut. He nodded. "Somebody waltzed into that bank yesterday afternoon, signed her name as Cissie Cordiner, produced the key to the box, opened it and waltzed out again."

"What?" Kelly asked in stunned disbelief. "My mother isn't here. She's in Cleveland."

"My guess is that it was Mavis and she's got those jewels right now. I called the police. They're opening the bank early so you can check. But I'd bet every dime I've got that those jewels are gone. I don't know how in hell she did it, but she did."

Kelly sagged and sat down weakly on the bed. He let go of her, but stood over her, his chest rising and falling as if he were ready to fight someone. She put her fingertips to her temples as if she could still her whirling thoughts."

"*Nobody* can get into a safety deposit box," she said. "It's not possible. You have to have a key. Your signature has to match the one on the file card."

"I'm aware of that," he said, throwing her T-shirts into the suitcase. "But somehow she figured out how to do it."

She shook her head. "I—I thought I'd misplaced the extra house key. I thought it was hanging by the door, but then it was gone. The first day she was here—" Kelly paused, remembering in disbelief "—she stumbled and caught herself against the door frame. She must have taken it then. And sometimes I thought things had been disturbed—just slightly. I kept thinking it was my imagination. But she—she's *been* in here. While I slept she was *in* here."

Zane scooped up a stack of shorts and tossed them into the suitcase. "Did your mother write anything about the safety deposit box? Did you have her cosign a card for it? Did she write and say she'd sent it back to the bank?"

Kelly looked at him, sick with betrayal. "Yes." Her voice was almost a whisper. "Just yesterday she wrote that she'd sent it to them. The card should have reached the bank at the same time her letter got to me. This morning—I—I thought that the letter was folded differently. I thought somebody had read it—I thought it had been you. Was it Mavis?"

"I don't read other people's mail," he said shortly.

"You read their manuscripts," she said, her voice as curt as his.

"That was different," he snapped. "And we're not discussing my shortcomings. We're discussing Mavis. So—she could have gotten in here, read the letter and known the bank had Cissie's signature on file. Right?"

"She knew about the jewels," Kelly said with a sick sense of wonder. "She had my house key, and she knew that if I was drugged I'd sleep so deeply she could come in and that the dog would never do anything. She could read the letters I wrote to my mother and the ones I'd received—she knew Mother was supposed to sign for the box, and she knew when the bank would get the card."

"Probably," he said, snapping shut the suitcase. "And she'd seen your mother's signature—on letters, I'd bet—enough to duplicate it. She could slip in here, lift your safety deposit key, walk into the bank, claim she was your mother here to help with the estate, forge the signature, which they would compare with the card, and get into the box. Nobody'd know. They've never seen your mother."

Kelly stared up at his stony features, still dazed. "A note from my mother disappeared. Mavis must have taken it to practice her signature. The people at the bank couldn't know she wasn't my mother. But my key? She stole my key to the box? I had coffee with her yesterday. She could have taken it when I went out of the room. Then I just—passed out almost. She must have drugged me again. And last night she insisted I take those cookies. She must have come in again last night when I slept—but why? And then I thought I heard her car leaving. What happened? I don't understand."

"You've been robbed, that's what," he said from between his teeth. "She must have taken the key yesterday morning and put it back last night. Hell, don't you see, Kelly? If you didn't miss the key, you'd never have known she'd had it. You wouldn't have known the jewels were gone until the end of the summer when you went to get them."

"They can't be gone," Kelly said desperately. She saw all her mother's dreams and her own vanishing like a wisp of smoke.

"Come on," he said with harsh resignation. Taking her elbow, he pulled her toward the front door.

Her knees felt gelatinous as he opened it. She looked at him, then at the worn welcome mat on the porch. The corner of a pink envelope protruded from under it.

"Go ahead," he said. "Look."

She knelt and lifted the corner of the mat. Lying beneath it was the pink envelope with her name scrawled across it. With unsteady fingers she ripped it open. It read:

Darling Kelly,
I just got word that my brother in Kansas is sick and

needs me. I must fly! I'll be back as soon as I can. You'll be hearing from me! After all, I want those pussycats! Take care, dear.

                                           Love, Mavis

Kelly stared up helplessly into Zane's eyes. "She's gone," she said, her voice shaking. She turned back toward the house. "The key. I want to see if the safety deposit key's there."

Zane followed her. She snapped open her purse, drew out her wallet and looked inside. "The key's still here," she breathed. "Maybe you're wrong."

His features grew harder than before. "I told you, Kelly, she put it back. So you wouldn't suspect. I think the jewels are gone. And she is, too."

"If she really took them . . ." She couldn't finish; she was almost nauseous with apprehension. Three hundred thousand dollars, she thought. The money that would have allowed Cissie to travel and be carefree for once in her hardworking life. The money that would have let Kelly have the freedom to write. She desperately needed that freedom, because she had to start everything over. Zane had made that all too clear to her.

She looked into his eyes again. She couldn't read them. She couldn't detect so much as a scrap of emotion. "Maybe the jewels aren't really gone." She breathed the words as if they were a prayer.

BUT PRAYERLIKE as they might have been, they did no good. When Zane drove her to the bank, a solemn president, a sleepy-looking teller, and two detectives watched as she opened the safety deposit box. It was empty.

The jewels were gone. They had vanished and Mavis Pruer had vanished with them.

The sweet little plain-faced lady who baked things, the small, harmless white-haired woman with the broken leg, was a thief and forger accomplished enough to do what everyone had said was impossible: breach the security of the safety-deposit-box system and walk off with a fortune.

AFTER KELLY AND ZANE had both given statements to the police, he took her to a little café on the square to buy her a cup of coffee.

"I still don't understand," Kelly said wanly. "Why didn't she get the jewels from Jimmie?"

"She probably came here to do just that," he said without emotion. "But he was dead."

"I mean why didn't she get them from him the summer before? In the first place?"

"Maybe she tried. She could have left in a hurry because somebody was on her trail. She probably came here originally to hide. This isn't the first time this woman's broken the law. She's obviously a professional. She's probably been doing things like this for years."

Kelly was silent. She didn't know how she would tell Cissie of the terrible loss. She leaned her elbows on the table and covered her eyes with her hands.

"Look," Zane said, his voice harsh again, "they'll probably catch her. You'll get the jewels back. Don't worry. In the meantime, I told you, I'll buy the blasted house. I can sell it to somebody else. It's no big deal. And you won't go home empty-handed."

"I won't go home at all," she said, shaking her head stubbornly, but keeping her eyes hidden. "It's not just the house. I have to find homes for those cats. *And* the dog."

Kelly thought of Pollyanna with a mixture of fondness, grief and resentment. The dog had repeatedly let a thief walk into her house, had probably wagged and danced and smiled with pleasure. Yet she couldn't hate the dog. The animal's only flaw was that she loved too much.

"I'll take care of that, too," he said grimly. "Everything."

"I don't want your charity," she protested, and she didn't. She wanted no favors from him, nothing except to be left alone. She raised her head and her gaze met his rebelliously.

"It isn't charity," he said, his lip curled. "It's for my own peace of mind. You're a city kid. You don't belong here. You need to go home and live your safe little life with your mother. You've been drugged, nearly drowned and robbed since you've been here."

Her face burned, and she pushed the empty coffee cup away. "I—" she began.

But he cut her off. "What's more," he said with a weary scowl, "it's not enough that you attracted a thief, you've also attracted that weirdo Hardesty, and I'm not, repeat, *am not* going to sit around worrying what he might do. Your mother wouldn't want you in that situation, Jimmie wouldn't want it, and I, by all that's holy, don't want it."

The tears she had fought all morning sprang to her eyes, but she fought them back. "First, don't call me a 'kid.' Second, I can take care of myself—"

The quirk of his mouth grew crueler. "You're a kid to me, and I don't want you around. Can you get that through your head? It would be an infinite relief to me if you'd just get out. I'm a professional with work to do, and you're an amateur screwing up my life."

She took a deep, quavering breath. A sickening new realization stole over her. "I know—I know that you have every right to be angry. I misjudged you. Mavis forged my mother's handwriting, and she must have forged Jimmie's, too. She must have made up those things in the letter, but why? Why did she do it? She *had* real letters from him. And she must have stolen some of his writing paper off the desk and changed the end of that one—"

Her words had no more effect on him than if he had been made of stone. She could tell from the set of his face that he'd read the letters she had given him.

"It was Jimmie's handwriting," she said helplessly. "It *seemed* to be."

"My God," he said, looking at her in contempt and shaking his head. "I read those things this morning. How could you believe such tripe? It didn't even sound like Jim. He'd never say anything like that—about anyone. Jim had his flaws, but he wasn't a hypocrite and he didn't slander friends. Didn't you *know* the man? Don't you know *me?* Have you ever really seen me? I don't think so. All you've ever seen is your own prejudice."

Aching regret surged through her. "She *lied.* Jim must have told her about you. She must have known that you looked out for his interests. She must have been—afraid of you. You were probably the last sort of person she wanted around. So she lied."

He narrowed his eyes. "The point isn't that she lied. The point is you were so damned eager to believe her. You never asked me. Not *once.* You just believed everything she dished up. But that's your style, isn't it? Don't find things out for yourself. Don't trust your feelings. Take everything secondhand. It's safer."

She blinked, stiffened her jaw and ferociously willed the tears to go away. He couldn't have said anything that hurt her more deeply because what he said was true. She had believed horrible lies about him, never questioning them. She had never confronted him or allowed him to defend himself.

"Go home to Mama," he said, his eyes cold. "Write your tidy little stories and live your tidy little life. Don't worry about the jewels. Odds are you'll get them back."

He stood, tossing money on the table to pay for their coffee. "Come on, kid," he said. "It's a long drive to Cleveland."

KELLY WENT HOME. Zane's prediction about the jewels came true; police in Missouri picked Mavis up less than a week after the theft. She not only had the jewels, but a considerable amount of cash she'd received for an insurance fraud—Mavis was only pretending to have a leg injury.

She hadn't bothered to return the door key she had pilfered from Kelly; it was still in her purse. Further damning evidence was found in Jimmie's house. Both Kelly's unwashed morning coffee cup and the leftover cookies contained traces of drugs.

Mavis had let herself into Jimmie's house repeatedly while Kelly slept. She had stolen the note from Cissie to practice forging Cissie's signature, and paper from Jimmie's tablet to forge the lies against Zane. Once she learned Cissie's signature was on file at the bank, her light fingers stole the safety deposit key from Kelly's purse. It was then a simple matter to get to the safety deposit box and the jewels. But to keep Kelly from suspecting, Mavis had drugged Kelly that morning, hoping to slip into the house to return the key.

But Terry Hardesty, with his spiteful watch on Kelly's house, had put a crimp on Mavis's plans. She'd worked around him neatly, too, drugging him, as well. But she wasn't able to get into Kelly's house until that night, when Kelly was drugged a second time by some of the same cookies Mavis had used to silence Terry Hardesty. Then she had slipped into the house, put the key back, written her farewell note and left, the jewels in her suitcase.

Mavis Pruer, it proved, was also known as Marvelle Prescott, and police were still trying to document the impossibly long list of her aliases and the equally long record of her convictions.

Zane, the police told Kelly in a telephone conversation, had been right about Mavis and Jimmie. Mavis had come to the lake the summer before to lie low after a forgery caper in Texas. She tried to befriend Jimmie, cleverly wheedling information from him bit by bit.

Once Mavis had learned of the jewels' existence, all she had to do was figure out how to get them. But even before her quick mind could find a way, she suspected authorities had picked up her trail. She had moved on quickly, leaving Jimmie safe for the time being.

In spite of her flight, police had caught her. She did a short stint in Houston for forgery, but once free, she couldn't resist coming back to get the jewels.

"All's well that ends well" was Cissie's philosophical attitude. Kelly told her about the theft, of course, but never about how much danger she had been in, and nothing about Zane.

Cissie, financially secure for the first time in her life, seemed happier than Kelly had ever seen her. She went to Hawaii, and while there met a widower from Cincinnati, a plump, courtly man who ran a bookstore. He talked about relocating in Cleveland, and Kelly sensed that her mother felt safe with a man for the first time in years. After all this time, romance was finally becoming real for Cissie.

Kelly finished her book of fables. This time she had given the book all she had to give: each brief story was steeped in its own emotion. Sales promised to be brisk, and advance reviews were excellent, with one critic calling the collection "a spellbinder, a new children's classic."

Kelly kept telling herself that she should have been happy, even ecstatic. Jimmie's bequest was safe and being used exactly as he wished. Cissie was relaxed and happy and seemed on the brink of a fulfilling new life. Kelly had done what she'd set out to do: she'd written a book of fantasies that children would like and adults admire.

But almost a year had passed since she'd left Arkansas, and still she could not keep thoughts of Zane from her mind. Why, she kept asking herself, had she been so snobbish to him at first about his work? By now she had read everything he'd written. He was a good writer, an excellent writer, possibly even a great one.

Cissie had criticized Kelly's new taste in reading until Kelly made her read *Her Demon Lover*. Then Cissie had said, "Well, the man can certainly write, but it's just not to my taste, thank you. To each his own." But she criticized no more.

If Kelly regretted her initial disdain for Zane's books, she regretted believing Mavis's lies even more. For that, she could not forgive herself. But she still couldn't understand why the woman had distorted the truth so viciously. Why had she feared Zane so, been so eager to turn Kelly against him?

The lies had been all too successful. They had turned Zane against Kelly, as well. Kelly unhappily admitted to herself that she supposed she was in love with Zane. The look of his face, the feel of his body, the sound of his voice haunted her, and when she read his books, she imagined she could feel his presence, as if the words were magic that could summon him to her, though never quite within her reach.

Mavis Pruer had poisoned her body, Kelly thought bitterly, and poisoned her mind, as well. Perhaps worst of all, she had poisoned a relationship that might have flowered into something wonderful, something enchanted.

No, Kelly would reprimand herself unhappily, that was only wishful thinking. He could never love her in return. He thought she was too young, too foolish, too troublesome. He had told her he would be glad to be rid of her and obviously he was. She had heard nothing from him since they'd parted. She had not tried to write to him. She was ashamed to.

She filled her days with work. She was writing a longer and more complicated book that mingled fantasy and reality more boldly than she had ever before attempted.

ONE MILD APRIL EVENING, Cissie's friend from Cincinnati came to take her to a performance of *Peter and the Wolf.* Kelly sat alone in the house at her desk in her tiny office.

She didn't give the ringing doorbell a second thought when she went to answer it, for she and Cissie had lived in the same neighborhood for years, and neighbors often dropped by in the evenings to visit with Cissie.

Kelly wore blue jeans and a pale yellow sweater. Her hair was pulled back in a French braid that was starting to come loose because she toyed with it sometimes when she sat at the typewriter. Stray tendrils floated free, but she didn't bother to smooth them back.

She thrust the pencil she had been holding behind her ear and went to the door. She had learned by now to be firm with people when she was writing. She would tell the caller that Cissie was gone, then say politely but purposefully that she had to get back to work.

She swung open the door, her practiced speech already forming on her lips.

Then she found she could not move her lips at all. Neither could she seem to move any other part of her body. She felt, momentarily, as frozen as if a wizard had turned her to stone.

Zane stood on her doorstep, the spring sky darkening behind him. She remained speechless, capable only of staring at him. He wore dark slacks and a heavy copper-colored wool sweater that made his shoulders seem more massive than usual. His stance was casual, his hands in his pockets, but the set of his face was so solemn it seemed tense.

It was the face she remembered so well, the high, flat cheekbones, the strong jaw, the stubborn chin, the deep-set eyes. His hair was longer than she remembered and browner, no longer streaked with the summer's sun.

He looked down into her eyes. He shook his head, as if something troubled him deeply.

"Zane?" she managed to breathe.

"I was haunted," he said, pain in his voice.

Her heart seemed to have lodged in her throat. "What?" she managed to whisper.

"I've been haunted," he repeated, the muscles of his jaw taut. "You've haunted me. Like a beautiful ghost I can't exorcise."

She wasn't even certain she had heard him correctly the blood was drumming so hard in her ears. "I—I—" she stammered. Surely he had not said what she'd thought she had heard. Mechanically she said, "Do you want to come in?"

"No," he answered, shaking his head again. "I want you to come out. It's like the first night of spring out here. Come out to meet it. Come meet it with me."

She nodded, unable to keep her eyes from his. They were as gray and as complicated with webs as she remembered, and complex emotions played behind them. He held out his hand to her. Wordlessly she took it. It was warm, hard, strong, and it throbbed with life against hers.

He led her onto the porch. Her mother's house was an old one, on a large corner lot with old trees at the porch's edge and one great lilac bush that was thick with lavender bloom.

He stopped beside it and took her other hand, as well. He stared down at her, shaking his head again. A bittersweet smile curved his mouth. "I hear your book is good, Kelly. It's all over the grapevine. You've got a winner on your hands. You did it. I'm proud of you."

"Thank you." Her voice shook. She was so happy to see him that she actually ached; it was too much happiness to bear. "I couldn't have done it without you," she said.

She was afraid he might vanish as suddenly as he had appeared. There were so many things she wanted to say that her words began spilling out in a rush. "I didn't think I'd ever forgive you for what you told me about my writing, but you were right. You said what had to be said."

"I said a lot of things I didn't think you'd ever forgive," he said. He tightened his hands around hers.

"We both said things," she breathed.

He nodded, his mouth going grim again. "Did we say too much? So much that we can never put it right?"

"I hope not," she said, and bit her lower lip, praying it was true. She knew she had forgiven him everything long ago. "Oh, I hope not."

He drew her nearer and gladly she went to his arms.

"I'm a lot older than you are," he said, his voice somber. "And I'm like Jim. Vietnam put a lot of miles on me. So did the business with my parents. I like a quiet life. I keep to myself, and I'm set in my ways. I fish too much, and I spend too much time thinking about vampires and ghosts and ghouls. It doesn't strike me that I'm much of a bargain. I've got money, but keep things simple, so I can never figure out what to spend it on. I already have everything I want. Everything in the world. Except you."

He laughed at himself. "Except you. I tried everything to get you out of my head. At first, I couldn't stop resenting that you believed all that rot Mavis made up. I couldn't understand why she'd even bother to do it—or why you'd fall for it."

"I don't know, either," Kelly said, tears glinting in her eyes. She gripped his upper arms, for, strong and solid as they were, she still feared he'd vanish.

Gently he brushed aside the tears that were forming in her eyes. "Don't cry," he said gruffly. "I understand—now. I told you about my father. How he was shot, how he was hurt. Well, Mavis was one of the couple that shot him. She couldn't have forgotten my name. It's the same as my father's, the man she went to jail for. It was almost twenty years ago, but she was afraid I'd remember her. And I would have, if I'd just had a little longer."

"She was one of the people your father stopped that night?" Kelly breathed. "How could she dare to come back?"

He paused, shaking his head. "It seems strange, but if anybody knows truth is stranger than fiction, it should be you and I. And people like Mavis have their circuits. Hers was Texas, Arkansas, Missouri, Tennessee—hitting here, hiding there, then back again. And she'd changed over the years, changed a lot.

"Nobody else recognized her at first, either," he said, concern in his eyes as he stared down at her. "But Barnstable—he's the sheriff—finally discovered that she was the same woman. That was about a hundred aliases ago for her."

He took a deep breath, as if it were painful to go on. "I didn't know until last month, when Barnstable told me. But that's why she didn't want me near her—or you. She didn't have to worry about me with Jim—I was gone that summer. But not when she came back. If I recognized her, I could have exposed her in a minute. So she worked overtime filling your head with lies."

Kelly found herself dazed and unsettled by the softness of his tone, the tenderness of his touch. "But I had no right to believe her—not without question," she said, shaking her head. "It was wrong."

"Kelly, Kelly," he said softly, taking her chin between his thumb and forefinger. "Don't you see? The woman was a spellbinder. A real spellbinder. She charmed Jimmie out of all kinds of information. When she saw she had to deal with you, instead, she already knew enough about you to know your weak spots. It was her business, knowing weak spots. She didn't want me butting in and ruining her plans. So she knew exactly which of your fears to play on, what buttons to push to keep us apart."

"But how could she come up with such schemes and lies so fast?" Kelly asked helplessly, unable to understand.

"I told you, Kelly—it's her business. Moving fast as a snake to strike a vulnerable spot, pretending, manipulating. Yes, I resented that you believed her. But when I found out who she really was, I realized just how much she must have lied to you. I also realized what I resented most wasn't that you believed her."

She looked up at him questioningly, her hands tightening apprehensively on his arms.

His face grew more solemn than before. "I under-stood—finally—what I really resented was that I didn't want to fall in love—not at all—but that I had. With you. I tried to fall back out. I tried for a year. It doesn't seem to work."

"No," Kelly said. "It doesn't, does it?" She understood perfectly and the knowledge made her breath catch in her throat. A chill evening breeze rustled across the lawn and she shivered.

His expression was pained, almost anguished. "I told you once that everybody's afraid of something. I was afraid of caring. I never wanted to let anybody close to me. Espe-cially after Vietnam, after that year of hell when everything happened. It seemed like that part of me was gone. But you made it live again. I couldn't let Mavis kill it again. And I won't. I love you, Kelly."

She was too full of emotion to speak. The cool breeze ca-ressed her again, and once more she trembled.

"Why are you shaking?" he asked, putting his hands on her shoulders. "Are you cold?"

"I'm afraid you'll disappear like a phantom," she said, shivering again. "That you're not really here and not really saying these things."

"I'm no ghost," he said, bending to her. "I'm flesh and blood." He kissed her, and Kelly's arms went around him, hungry to feel his touch again, to assure herself that he was real. He kissed her until everything else in the world seemed to fall away except him and happiness and the sweetness of desire.

At last he drew back, smiling down at her. "You could learn to stand a very quiet, very low-key, very private life in Arkansas?"

"I've already learned to," she said, smiling up at him. "I loved it as soon as I saw it. I've missed it."

"You could live with a man whose head will always be full of fantasies about werewolves and assorted goblins?"

She wound her arms happily around his neck. "Can you live with a woman whose head will always be full of fantasies about ladybugs and leprechauns?"

"We'll walk around the house, lost in our separate worlds, muttering and bumping into each other."

"It sounds wonderful," she said, smiling more happily. "I can't wait to mutter and bump. I want to mutter and bump for the rest of our lives."

"I want you to know," he said with a grin, "that I found a home for every one of those blasted cats. It was no more difficult than writing a thousand-page novel. But I did it."

"I knew you would," she said fondly. "You're a man of your word. And Pollyanna?"

His grin faded. "That takes some explaining."

In spite of Kelly's joy, fear constricted her chest. "Something happened to her? Oh, please don't say that—something happened?"

He shook his head and kissed the tip of her nose. "All that happened was that I kept her. My other dogs haven't forgiven me and probably never will. She prances around like a ballerina and tries to kiss them all the time. They're disgusted."

"You—with Pollyanna?" Kelly laughed in delight.

"I couldn't let her go. She reminded me of Jim, but more than that, she reminded me of you." His face went grimly unhappy. "But she made me remember you too well. All the time. Day in. Day out. I kept thinking, what am I going to do with this fool dog? She wasn't meant to be mine. She needs somebody else. And I knew who, because I need the same person. You. Every time I saw her I knew I needed you more. So here I am. She was finally good for something."

"She was always good for loving," Kelly teased gently, and kissed his chin.

His expression softened. "Yes. She was always good for that." He stroked her hair. "Oh, Kelly. I've had fantasies about you. And they weren't horrible. They were—something else."

"I've had fantasies about you, too," she admitted, nuzzling his neck. "And they weren't childish."

"Then let's explore them," he said, bending to kiss her again. "That's our sort of work, isn't it?"

"It's the job we were made to do," she said, then lost herself in the dizzying spell of his kiss.

FREE GIFT OFFER

To receive your free gift, send us the specified number of proofs-of-purchase from any specially marked Free Gift Offer Harlequin or Silhouette book with the Free Gift Certificate properly completed, plus a check or money order (do not send cash) to cover postage and handling payable to Harlequin/Silhouette Free Gift Promotion Offer. We will send you the specified gift.

FREE GIFT CERTIFICATE

ITEM	A. GOLD TONE EARRINGS	B. GOLD TONE BRACELET	C. GOLD TONE NECKLACE
# of proofs-of-purchase required	3	6	9
Postage and Handling	$1.75	$2.25	$2.75
Check one	☐	☐	☐

Name: _____

Address: _____

City: _____ State: _____ Zip Code: _____

Mail this certificate, specified number of proofs-of-purchase and a check or money order for postage and handling to: HARLEQUIN/SILHOUETTE FREE GIFT OFFER 1992, P.O. Box 9057, Buffalo, NY 14269-9057. Requests must be received by July 31, 1992.

PLUS—Every time you submit a completed certificate with the correct number of proofs-of-purchase, you are automatically entered in our MILLION DOLLAR SWEEPSTAKES! No purchase or obligation necessary to enter. See below for alternate means of entry and how to obtain complete sweepstakes rules.

MILLION DOLLAR SWEEPSTAKES
NO PURCHASE OR OBLIGATION NECESSARY TO ENTER

To enter, hand-print (mechanical reproductions are not acceptable) your name and address on a 3"×5" card and mail to Million Dollar Sweepstakes 6097, c/o either P.O. Box 9056, Buffalo, NY 14269-9056 or P.O. Box 621, Fort Erie, Ontario L2A 5X3. Limit: one entry per envelope. Entries must be sent via 1st-class mail. For eligibility, entries must be received no later than March 31, 1994. No liability is assumed for printing errors, lost, late or misdirected entries.

Sweepstakes is open to persons 18 years of age or older. All applicable laws and regulations apply. Sweepstakes offer void wherever prohibited by law. Prizewinners will be determined no later than May 1994. Chances of winning are determined by the number of entries distributed and received. For a copy of the Official Rules governing this sweepstakes offer, send a self-addressed, stamped envelope (WA residents need not affix return postage) to: Million Dollar Sweepstakes Rules, P.O. Box 4733, Blair, NE 68009.

HR1U

ONE PROOF-OF-PURCHASE
To collect your fabulous FREE GIFT you must include the necessary FREE GIFT proofs-of-purchase with a properly completed offer certificate.

FREE GIFTS WITH PURCHASE

(See center insert for details)

Following the success of WITH THIS RING,
Harlequin cordially invites you to enjoy the
romance of the wedding season with

BARBARA BRETTON
RITA CLAY ESTRADA
SANDRA JAMES
DEBBIE MACOMBER

A collection of romantic stories that celebrate the joy,
excitement, and mishaps of planning that special day
by these four award-winning Harlequin authors.

**Available in April at your favorite Harlequin
retail outlets.**